Contents

STRIPES PUBLISHING LIMITED
An imprint of the Little Tiger Group
1 Coda Studios, 189 Munster Road,
London SW6 6AW

A paperback original
First published in Great Britain in 2021

Imported into the EEA by Penguin Random House Ireland,
Morrison Chambers, 32 Nassau Street, Dublin D02 YH68

ISBN: 978-1-78895-319-1

A CIP catalogue record for this book is available from the British Library.

Printed and bound in the UK.

MIX
Paper from
responsible sources
FSC
www.fsc.org   FSC® C020471

The Forest Stewardship Council® (FSC®) is a global, not-for-profit
organization dedicated to the promotion of responsible forest management
worldwide. FSC defines standards based on agreed principles for
responsible forest stewardship that are supported by environmental, social,
and economic stakeholders. To learn more, visit www.fsc.org

10 9 8 7 6 5 4 3 2 1

The
Abandoned
Puppy

For Kitty

Chapter One

The littlest puppy whimpered quietly. The cardboard box had stopped bouncing up and down, but no one had come to get her out, and it was still so dark. She didn't like it. She didn't know where her mother was, and she was hungry.

She squeaked in frightened surprise as a low rumbling noise shook the box.

It seemed to be moving again, swinging and then sliding across the floor. Her two brothers slammed into her, knocking her against the side of the box as the car went round a sharp corner.

The journey seemed to go on for a very long time, but she couldn't even curl up for a sleep. Every time she managed to get comfortable, the box would slide around again, and they'd all be on top of each other. It was nothing like their rough-and-tumble puppy play in the big basket at home. This hurt, and they couldn't go and snuggle up against their mother when they wanted the game to stop.

Pressed into the furthest corner, the puppy scrabbled anxiously against her brothers. They were sitting on her again! Then she realized that they'd stopped – the box wasn't sliding around any more. Her brothers stood up cautiously. They listened, flinching a little at the creaky wheeze of the car boot opening. Then the box swung up into the air, and was dropped down with a heavy thud.

They heard footsteps, hurrying away. And then they were left alone.

"Are you ready to go, Zoe?" Auntie Jo was standing at the front door to their terraced house, wearing her wellies and her Redlands Animal Shelter fleece.

"Yes!" Zoe dashed down the hallway, stuffing the packet of dried apricots that Mum had found in the back of the cupboard into her lunchbox. She and Mum had both forgotten she'd need packed lunches this week, so Zoe's lunch was a bit random. Still, she really liked golden syrup sandwiches!

"Where's your big sister?" Auntie Jo asked, peering down the hallway into the kitchen.

"She's still asleep." Zoe shook her head. "Kyra thinks I'm mad getting up early to come with you when I don't have to."

"Well, if you stayed at home with your sister all day you'd just end up watching TV for the whole of the Easter holidays!" Mum called out. "You'll have a much better time at the shelter!"

"I heard that!" Kyra's voice floated down from upstairs. "I'm not asleep and I'm not watching TV. I'm revising! In bed! See you later, Auntie Jo. I'll come and pick Zoe up."

Kyra had her GCSEs coming up, so she was revising as hard as she could. Zoe was really glad that Auntie Jo had said she could help out at the shelter – she normally only got to help out after school. It would have been boring being stuck at home with Kyra, and Mum couldn't afford to take any time off work. Sometimes when they were off school she got to spend the day with her friend Becca, but Becca had gone to her gran's in Scotland for the fortnight.

"Thanks for letting me come for the whole day," Zoe said to Auntie Jo, as they walked to the shelter, which was about ten minutes from Zoe's house.

"That's all right!" Auntie Jo grinned at her. "I'm not going to be letting you off lightly, you know. I've got a long list of jobs for you to do, starting with cleaning out the dogs' runs, then bathing the cats, and maybe even knitting some bodywarmers for the guinea pigs..." She looked down at Zoe's worried face. "It's all right, I'm teasing you, Zo! There will be loads of useful stuff you can do, I promise, but it'll be mostly exercising the dogs, if it's not too wet. They don't get walked as much on the weekends, because that's when we get most of our visitors. They'll all be desperate for a good run around."

Redlands was quite a small shelter, but it took in every kind of animal. The staff did their best to get them all rehomed but it wasn't always easy. Auntie Jo had been working there for three years now, ever since she'd gone to the shelter to get a cat and come home with Barney, her gorgeous tabby. She had been working as a receptionist at the local vet back then. That's how she knew all about Redlands. She'd ended up volunteering to help out at the shelter in her spare time. Then, when a job had come up as manager, she'd jumped at the chance. Zoe had been delighted too.

"You're so lucky, getting to be at the shelter every day, and see all the dogs," Zoe sighed. "I'm definitely going to work somewhere like Redlands when I'm older. Or maybe I'll be a vet," she added thoughtfully.

Auntie Jo smiled at her. "It is a lovely job at the shelter," she agreed. "But it does have its sad bits too. Sometimes it makes me so angry the way people don't look after their animals properly. And it isn't always the owner's fault either. Sometimes they really love their pets, but they just can't care for them in the same way any more. That's really heartbreaking." She sighed. "I just want to take them all home with me. But four cats is quite enough."

Having just Barney the tabby hadn't lasted very long. Auntie Jo was a sucker for big fluffy cats.

"Mmmm. So, did anybody take a

dog or cat home over the weekend?" Zoe asked. She loved hearing about the new homes the animals went to. She liked to imagine herself into some of the stories Auntie Jo told. She would have loved to have had a dog from the shelter, but she knew they couldn't. It wouldn't be fair to leave it all alone in their house while Mum was at work, and Kyra wasn't really a dog fan either. She'd been chased across the park by a huge Bernese Mountain Dog when she was about four. She and Mum had been on their way to nursery, and Kyra had been on her scooter. The dog had only wanted to be friendly, but Kyra hadn't known that, and she'd fallen off trying to get away from him. She'd been scared of dogs ever since.

"Edward got chosen this weekend!" said Auntie Jo. "Finally! I'm so pleased, Zoe. I thought he'd never find a home!" Zoe grinned. Edward was one of the older dogs – a bulldog. A lot of people seemed to think that they were weird-looking. Everyone always wanted a cute little puppy but Edward had such a sweet nature.

"An elderly man came in," Auntie Jo went on. "He wanted Edward straightaway. He said that he'd always had bulldogs, and Edward was a smasher. That's what he called him – a little smasher!"

Zoe giggled. "I hope he isn't. He is a bit clumsy. He does bump into things."

Auntie Jo laughed. "One of the staff went round and did a home visit, because Mr Johnson was so keen to take Edward straightaway. She said it looked perfect. A nice bit of garden, and near a park for good walks. She reckoned Edward and Mr Johnson were a perfect match – both of them on the elderly side. You know Edward never liked walking very fast!"

Zoe nodded. She'd taken Edward

round the park with Auntie Jo and a couple of the other dogs from the shelter before. It was the slowest walk she'd ever been on!

"Lucky Edward. And lucky Mr Johnson," Zoe said. "I bet they're having such a lovely time." She wrapped her arm through Auntie Jo's, and leaned against her with a sigh. "I know we can't, but I do wish I could have a dog of my own..."

Chapter Two

The box seemed to be getting colder and colder. The April night had been frosty, and the puppies had huddled together to keep warm. They weren't used to being outside at night and there was only the thin cardboard box between them and the concrete steps. They had always slept in their comfortable basket, snuggled up next to their mother. The cold was a frightening shock.

The smallest of the three, the tiny girl puppy, woke up first. She was miserably stiff, the cold aching inside her, and she scrabbled worriedly at the cardboard under her paws. Her two brothers were still asleep, curled up together, but somehow during the night she had rolled away from them. Now she was on her own in the corner of the box, shivering and hungry.

She tried to scratch at the side of the box, wondering if she could get out, and somehow find her way back to her mother.

But even her claws hurt this morning, and she felt weak and sleepy. Too feeble to claw a hole in the side of a box.

She still didn't understand what had happened. Why had they been taken away from their mother, and their warm basket? Was someone going to come and get them, and take them back to her? When they'd been put into the box, she'd heard her mother barking and whining – she hadn't wanted them to go any more than they had. The littlest puppy had a horrible feeling that they might not be going back.

Zoe and her aunt were nearly at the shelter. Zoe could feel herself speeding up. She loved it when they got to be the ones who opened up at Redlands – it was a real treat, and usually only happened if Auntie Jo let her come and help on a Saturday. She knew that all the animals would be excited to see someone after the night on their own. The dogs would be the most obvious about it, jumping about and scrabbling at the wire mesh on the front of their pens, and barking like mad. But even the cats, who usually liked to be more stand-offish, would spring up from their baskets, and come to see who was there. The shelter had a big pen full of guinea pigs at the moment, so there would be mad squeaking from them as well.

Auntie Jo was searching in her bag for the keys, so it was Zoe who first noticed that there was something strange on the front steps.

"What's that?" she asked curiously, frowning at what looked like a box in front of the main door to the shelter.

Auntie Jo looked up from the bunch of keys. "What?"

"There. On the steps. Maybe someone's donated food to the shelter, Auntie Jo!" People did bring in pet food for the animals occasionally, Zoe had seen them. "It's funny that they didn't bring it in when there was someone who could say thank you, though."

"Mmmm…" Auntie Jo was walking faster now, the keys dangling forgotten in her hand.

"What's the matter?" Zoe asked. She could see that her aunt looked worried.

"People leave us other things too, Zoe," Auntie Jo sighed. "It might be an abandoned animal in that box. If it is, I suppose that at least they've brought it to us, but I hate it when they just leave it like that."

Zoe felt her eyes filling with tears. The box was just a box, a shabby cardboard one. How could someone stuff a cat or a dog in there, and then just leave it? It was so mean!

They hurried up the steps, and sat down slowly, one on either side of the lid. Auntie Jo took a deep breath. "I never get used to this," she murmured, as she started to unfold the flaps on the top. "It's been such a cold night. Look, there's frost on the top. If there's something inside, I hope it hasn't been in there long."

There was a feeble scrabbling noise from inside the box, and Zoe caught her breath. "There is something inside there!"

Auntie Jo frowned at the box. "Yes.

And I'm being silly, Zo. We should take the box inside. We don't want whoever's in here getting scared and leaping out."

Zoe nodded. "Good idea. Shall I take it?" she asked hopefully. "You unlock the door."

Carefully, Zoe slipped her hands underneath the box, shivering as she touched the clammy, cold cardboard. Whoever was in it must have spent a miserably cold night. She heaved the box up, and felt something inside it wriggle.

There was a worried little squeak, and a yap.

"It's OK," she whispered. "We're just taking you into the shelter. It'll be nice and warm in there. Well, warmer than out here, anyway."

Auntie Jo had unlocked the doors now, and she was just turning off the alarm. She held the door open for Zoe, and they hurried into the reception area, putting the box down on one of the chairs.

"I think it's a dog," Zoe told her aunt. "I definitely heard a yapping noise. But it can't be a very big dog, the box hardly weighed anything at all."

"Let's see." Auntie Jo lifted the flaps of the box – it was meant to hold packets of chocolate biscuits, Zoe noticed – and they both peered in.

Staring anxiously up at them were three tiny brown-and-white puppies.

Chapter Three

The littlest puppy flinched back against the side of the box. She was still so tired from being bounced and shaken around, and now the light was flooding in, after hours of being shut in the dark. It hurt her eyes and she whimpered unhappily. Her bigger, stronger brothers recovered more quickly, bouncing up to see what was happening, and where they were. But the little girl puppy pressed her nose into the corner of the box, hiding away from the light. She was too cold and tired to get up, anyway.

Zoe and her aunt gazed inside, and Zoe pushed her hand into Auntie Jo's. She'd never seen such little puppies at the shelter, she was sure. They were the smallest pups she'd ever seen anywhere. "Oh my goodness, three of them," murmured Auntie Jo.

"They're so tiny," Zoe whispered. "They can hardly weigh anything at all."

Auntie Jo nodded. "Mmmm. They're far too young to be away from their mother, really. They can only be a few weeks old. Well done for keeping quiet, Zo. We don't want to scare them.

They may not be used to seeing different people."

The puppies were looking up at Zoe and Auntie Jo uncertainly. One of the boy puppies scrabbled hopefully at the side of the box, clearly wanting to be lifted out.

"Well, he's not shy," Auntie Jo laughed quietly.

Very gently, she slipped her hands into the box, and lifted out the puppy.

He wagged his stubby little tail, and licked her fingers. "Yes, you're a darling, aren't you?" She turned to Zoe.

"They must be starving if they've been in this box all night. Now I can see him properly, I don't think this little boy can be more than four weeks old. He's probably only just been weaned from his mother. They should be having four or five meals a day, and a bit of their mum's milk still."

Zoe giggled. "That's why he's trying to eat your fingers..." Then she looked worriedly down into the box. "Auntie Jo, what about the little puppy in the corner? Is she OK? She isn't moving like the other two."

Her aunt sighed. "No, she isn't... We'd better have a look at her. Can you bring the box along to one of the puppy pens? Then we'll have somewhere cosy for them to curl up, and we can mix up some puppy milk. Maybe a little bit of Weetabix mixed in it too. We'll have to see what they think. They may not have had any solid food yet."

Zoe gently lifted up the box, with two puppies still in it, and followed her aunt through to the main shelter area, where all the pens were. Dogs jumped up excitedly as they came past, barking for their breakfast, and for someone to come and make a fuss of them. Zoe looked down worriedly at the two puppies in the box. The bigger one – she was pretty sure it was another boy – was now standing up, balancing carefully on plump little paws, and listening to the new and exciting noises. He looked up curiously at Zoe – the only person he could see at the moment.

Maybe he thinks it's me barking! Zoe thought to herself, smiling down at him.

But her smile faded as she looked over to his litter-mate. The tiny puppy was still curled miserably in the corner of the box. She didn't seem to want to get up and see what was going on at all.

"We'll put them in here – nice and close to the kitchen," Auntie Jo said, opening one of the pen doors, and crooning to the puppy snuggled in the crook of her arm. "I'm pretty sure we've got a big tin of that powdered puppy milk replacement left," Auntie Jo murmured. "And some of the made-up bottles. I'd better order some more though."

She sat down on the floor in the pen

with the puppy in her arms, and Zoe put the box down next to her, kneeling beside it. "Should we take the others out?" she asked, looking at the boy puppy, who was clawing excitedly at the side of the box now.

Auntie Jo nodded. "Be careful though, Zoe. Don't scare them. They might not be very big, but puppies can still nip if they're frightened. Get the bigger puppy out first, then we can let him explore with this one, while we see what's the matter with the tiny one."

Zoe reached in and picked up the puppy, who was still standing up against the side of the box. He wriggled and yapped excitedly and when she put him down on her lap, he squirmed around eagerly, trying to see everything in the pen. Then he nuzzled Zoe's fingers, and wriggled carefully down the leg of her jeans, making for the floor. He obviously just wanted to go exploring this new place.

The other boy puppy was still snuggled on Auntie Jo's lap, looking around curiously, but not quite confident enough to go marching around like his brother.

"Try just giving the little one a gentle stroke," Auntie Jo advised. "Don't go straight in and pick her up. She isn't looking at us, and she'd get a shock."

Zoe reached in and ran one finger down the puppy's silky back. The brown fur was so soft, but she didn't feel as warm as her brother. "She's pretty cold," Zoe said, glancing round at Auntie Jo. "Even just touching her. And she's sort of floppy."

Auntie Jo bit her lip. "She's suffered more being out all night because she's smaller. Here, put this on your lap, Zoe." She lifted a soft fleece blanket out of a padded basket in the corner of the pen. "Then lift her out carefully, and wrap her up. Just loosely. And keep your hands round her to warm her up a bit."

Zoe nodded, and gently cupped one hand around the puppy. The tiny dog shivered a little as she felt Zoe's fingers, and turned her head slightly. But she was just too weak to look up. Zoe slipped the other hand underneath her, and lifted her out on to the blanket. She swathed it round the puppy, stroking her gently through the folds.

"OK, little one," Auntie Jo murmured to the puppy on her lap. "I need to go and get your sister a hot-water bottle. And make up some milk for you guys. Hmm? Want to go and see this nice basket?" She lifted the puppy in, and stroked him for a few seconds until he got used to being somewhere new. Then she got up slowly. The other boy puppy trotted over to the basket too, nosing affectionately at his brother.

"Those two seem fine," she said, sounding relieved. "And I'm sure they'll be even perkier once they've had something to eat."

Zoe looked up at her. "What about this one?" Her voice wobbled. "You don't think she's going to be all right?"

Auntie Jo sighed. "We don't know yet. She seems very weak. I'm going to call Sam at the vet's and ask if she'll come over as soon as she can and have a look at them all. Are you OK with them for a minute, while I get a hot water bottle for the little one?"

Zoe nodded, still gently rubbing the puppy through the blanket. She wished she could feel her moving. The puppy felt like a saggy little bean bag, slumped on her lap. Carefully she moved the blanket from round the puppy's head, peering down at her. Her eyes were closed, and her pink tongue was slightly sticking out of her mouth. It looked dry, Zoe thought worriedly. Auntie Jo had better hurry up with that puppy milk. She hoped they'd be able to persuade the pup to drink it. She didn't look like she wanted to make the effort to do anything just at the minute.

"Here's the hot water bottle," Auntie Jo said, hurrying back. "I've wrapped it up so it isn't too hot."

"Do we lie her on top of it?" Zoe asked, starting to lift the puppy off her lap.

"No, that would be too hot. I'm going to put it at the side of the basket, then she can snuggle next to it. We'll just have to keep an eye on her brothers, and make sure they don't nudge her away."

"Maybe we ought to put her in a pen on her own," Zoe said doubtfully. "They're a lot bigger than she is. They might push her around."

"I'd rather keep them together if we

can. She's already lost her mother, and her home. Her brothers are the only security she knows. Also, if we separate her, she might find it difficult to manage being around other dogs when she's bigger."

Zoe nodded as she laid the puppy close to the hot water bottle. "We don't want her to be lonely," she agreed.

"I've started to warm up some puppy milk. I'll just go and get it, and we can see what they think." Auntie Jo nipped into the kitchen, and came back with a shallow metal tray of the special puppy milk. "Hopefully they won't tip this over," she explained to Zoe, who was looking at the tray in surprise – it looked like something her mum would make chocolate brownies in.

The two boy puppies had been nosing around the edges of the pen, trying to explore, but as soon as Auntie Jo put the tray down, they galloped over to see what it was – so fast that they got tangled up, and fell over each other. They struggled to their feet, mock-growling, and then scurried up to the tray, sniffing at it excitedly. It only took seconds before they were eagerly lapping, burying their tiny muzzles in the milk and splashing it around.

"They must have had milk from bowls before," Zoe said, watching them and giggling.

"Maybe. Or else they're just fast learners," said Auntie Jo. "I don't think we need to worry about them not feeding. I'll mix a bit of Weetabix into the next lot." But she was frowning. "I'd really hoped that the smell would wake the little one up, but she doesn't seem to have noticed. We'll have to try feeding it to her by the bottle."

Zoe nodded. "Shall I put her on my lap?" she asked hopefully. She'd loved holding the puppy before, and trying to warm her up. Even though it was frightening that the puppy was ill, it felt really special to be the ones trying to make her better.

"Yes. Unwrap her, and we'll try to get her to take a bottle. I brought one just in case." Auntie Jo took a baby's bottle with a cap out of the pocket of her fleece, and sat down next to Zoe. "She's still so sleepy..."

The puppy was really floppy now, and she didn't wriggle when Zoe unwrapped her. Auntie Jo held the teat of the bottle up to her mouth, but she didn't seem to notice it. She certainly didn't start sucking, as Zoe had hoped she would. She only turned her head away a little, as though Auntie Jo nudging the bottle against her mouth was annoying.

"She doesn't want it," Zoe said worriedly. "Is there anything else we can give her?"

"We could try using a syringe..." Auntie Jo said thoughtfully. "We can poke it into the corner of her mouth, and try and trickle it in." But Zoe could see that her aunt was doubtful about the puppy ever feeding at all.

"What about..." Zoe brushed her fingers against the teat, letting a few drops of milk ooze out of the tiny hole on to her fingers. It was thick and yellowish, not like ordinary milk at all. Holding her breath, she stroked her milky fingers across the puppy's mouth, letting the milk run on to the dry, pink tongue.

The puppy shivered with surprise, and the little tongue darted out, licking Zoe's fingers.

"She likes it!" Zoe squeaked.

Auntie Jo smiled. "Quick, you take the bottle. Squeeze a little out on to the end of the teat, and dribble it into her mouth."

The puppy licked eagerly at the teat this time, and when Zoe pushed it gently against her mouth, she sucked, harder and harder, until she was slurping messily at the milk.

And then, at last, she opened her dark eyes, and stared up at Zoe.

Chapter Four

To: Becca
From: Zoe
Subject: Puppies

Hi Becca!

Hope you're having a good time at your gran's. Sorry I've not mailed you for a couple of days. Been sooooo busy! I went to the shelter with Auntie Jo on Monday, and someone had abandoned three puppies in a box on the front steps!!! (Here's a photo.

Auntie Jo took it on her phone. Aren't they gorgeous?) It was a box that was meant to be for chocolate biscuits, so we've called the two boys Choc and Biscuit, and the little girl puppy Cookie. She's really lovely. When we first found them she was really weak and Auntie Jo told me afterwards she wasn't sure she was going to make it. We're giving her milk from a bottle because she won't eat mashed-up Weetabix, even though her two brothers love it! (You should see them eating, it goes everywhere, we have to wash them afterwards!) But some of it must be going inside them - they're getting fatter every day! Cookie is definitely getting bigger too, and she likes me to carry her round everywhere! I've got lots more photos that Mum's printed out for me, I'll show you when you get back.

Love Zoe xxxxxxxxxxxxx

I can't believe you found puppies! You are so lucky. Gran's is OK but it's a bit cold as it's by the sea. I went paddling and my toes almost fell off.

Will the puppies get new owners from the shelter? How old are they? I wish I could come and see them. Guess what? Mum and Dad say we can definitely have a dog (you know they wouldn't make up their minds before). But now they say we have to go slow and make sure we find the right dog! Aaargh! I really want to have a dog NOW! When I get back please ask your auntie if I can come and see the puppies. Maybe one of them could be our dog!!!

From Becca xxxxxxxxxxx

Zoe read Becca's reply to her email, smiling to herself. Becca wrote emails just like she talked. But her smile faded a little as she read on to the end. Becca was so lucky to be allowed a dog. Zoe had been talking to Auntie Jo about the puppies today at the shelter. They'd been weighing them to check that they were eating enough, which was quite difficult because Choc, Biscuit and Cookie saw no reason why they should stand still on top of the scales, and just kept bouncing around. In the end, Auntie Jo had made a guess at their weights, but she said they were definitely getting heavier, which was the main thing.

Then they'd taken five minutes just to play with the puppies – it seemed like fun, rather than work, but Zoe knew it was actually really important. If the puppies didn't ever get played with, they wouldn't know how to behave with their new owners.

"How could anyone have abandoned them?" Zoe said sadly, watching Biscuit and Choc bombing up and down the pen, chasing after a ball. Cookie was scampering after them, not quite brave enough or fast enough to take the ball off her brothers, but having just as much fun. "They're so gorgeous, all of them. How could anyone be so mean?"

Auntie Jo sighed. "Well, at least they brought them here. It was a start."

"But they left them out in the cold all night!"

"Mmm. Some people just don't think. The puppies were probably an accident – they hadn't had the mum spayed, and then maybe the owners felt they couldn't afford to buy all the puppy food, and take the puppies to the vet for vaccinations. Dogs are expensive to look after." She reached over to put her arm round Zoe's shoulders. "Don't think about it, Zo. The puppies were lucky they ended up here, so they've got all of us looking after them. We're going to turn them into lovely, well-behaved dogs, and make sure they only go to fab owners. They won't remember their horrible start."

"I hope not," Zoe whispered, with a tiny sigh. Auntie Jo's words were meant to make her feel better. She knew the puppies would need to leave the shelter in a few weeks, but she'd been trying not to think about it too much. She'd only known them for a few days, but they were so sweet, Cookie especially. If they could stay at the shelter for a bit longer, she'd be able to keep on looking after them... But that wasn't fair. They needed proper homes.

Reading the exciting news in Becca's email had made her think about having to say goodbye to the puppies all over again...

To: Becca
From: Zoe
Subject: Puppies

Hi Becca

Auntie Jo thinks the puppies were about four weeks old when we found them, so now they're five weeks. They can't go to new homes until they're about eight weeks old. I'm sure you can come and see them, I'll ask Auntie Jo. You're so lucky getting a dog!

I hope your mum and dad decide on one soon. See you back at school in a week!

Love Zoe xx

It wasn't as friendly as her emails to Becca usually were, but Zoe was feeling sad. She stared at her computer screen, not really seeing the cute photo of Cookie that she had set as her wallpaper.

"What's up?"

Zoe jumped. She hadn't heard Mum come in at all. "Nothing... I was just thinking about the puppies. I'm going to miss them so much when they get rehomed." She gulped. "Especially Cookie."

Mum nodded. "She is gorgeous." Zoe had shown Mum the puppies one afternoon at the shelter, when Mum had come to pick her up. "I think it's her eyes. She's got such a little face, it makes her eyes look huge, and then she's got those lovely whiskery eyebrows. Has Auntie Jo worked out what breed they are yet?"

Zoe giggled and shook her head. "Nope. Everyone at Redlands thinks they're something different. Auntie

Jo reckons maybe there's some Jack Russell in them and maybe some Cockapoo too. But we might not be able to tell until they're bigger. Almost grown-up. And we won't have them then, will we? So we'll never know." She sniffed, and Mum hugged her.

"But you knew they'd have to go to new homes, Zo! All the animals at the shelter do. You've never got this upset before."

"I know. Maybe it was because we found them – and feeding Cookie with the bottle has made her special to me, Mum." Zoe smiled proudly. "I got her to take some puppy mix and milk in a bowl this morning. Auntie Jo was really pleased, she said that she'd thought Cookie was going to have to be on bottles for ever!"

"Your Auntie Jo ought to be paying you wages!" Mum sighed. "I know you love it at the shelter, but maybe you should have a couple of days off from helping out? Do something else? I bet Kyra could take enough time away from her revision to take you shopping. Or the cinema?"

Zoe looked horrified. "Oh no, Mum! I've got to keep going. I've got to help Cookie get on with the solid food. It's really important."

Her mum gave her a worried look. "Well, I suppose so…"

Chapter Five

"It sounds like the best Easter holidays ever!" Becca sighed enviously.

Zoe smiled at her as they walked into their classroom. "It was fab. I really missed going to the shelter this morning. I was looking forward to seeing you, but apart from that I could have done without school!"

"Me too, but I can't see my mum

letting me have the day off because I needed to go and visit the world's cutest puppies…" Becca flopped down into her chair, and glanced over at the board. "Numeracy problems! Great start to the new term…" She got out her maths book, but went on talking in a whisper. "So is Cookie properly weaned now? She's eating real puppy food?"

Zoe nodded. "Yup, they all still have a bit of milk, but they've started drinking water too. And Cookie's really catching up with Biscuit and Choc. I don't think she'll ever be quite as big as they are, but she's doing OK. I brought the photos Mum printed out – I'll show you at break— Ssh! – Mrs Allan's watching us right now." She stopped talking and tried to look like she was concentrating on the problems that Mrs Allan had put on the board for them. Their teacher was usually lovely, but she always got extra strict when they came back after the holidays – as though she thought they needed to remember what school was like!

Zoe showed the photos to Becca and some of the other girls in her class at break time, and everyone said how gorgeous the puppies were. Lots of the girls said they were going to ask their mums and dads if they could come to the shelter and see the puppies, and maybe even adopt one of them. Zoe knew that most of her friends wouldn't be allowed to – Lucy already had two dogs at home, for a start! But the more people who came to see the puppies the better. However much Zoe hated the thought of them leaving the shelter, she wanted them to have the very best of homes.

That afternoon, Auntie Jo had arranged to nip out from the shelter and pick Zoe up from school. Mum was going to fetch her after she finished work. Zoe got changed quickly in the staff loos – Mum hated her getting her school uniform messy – and then ran to see Cookie and the others.

Cookie was curled up in their basket, watching her brothers playing tug-of-war with a bit of old rope that someone had given them. They'd had it since the morning, and it was their new favourite toy. Bits of it were scattered all over the pen. She sighed a little, and rested her nose on her paws, wondering where Zoe was. Zoe had played with her every day since they'd come here from their old home. Actually, the little puppy couldn't remember much of where they'd lived before they'd been at the shelter. The only thing she was sure of was that their mother had been at the old place. She still wondered what had happened, and why they had been taken away, but she didn't mind, because now she had Zoe.

Except that today she didn't, and she didn't understand why. Zoe always fed her and her brothers. Zoe made a special fuss of them, even though she wasn't feeding milk from her lap any more. Zoe still brought the food bowls, and watched to make sure that she was eating properly. Zoe even stopped Choc and Biscuit from trying to take her food if they finished theirs first.

Today the other lady had brought their food - Jo, the one who was always with Zoe. Jo had said nice things, and she'd stroked her, and said how good she was. But it wasn't the same.

Cookie's little ears pricked up sharply. Someone was running along the passage

between the
pens - someone
with small, light
footsteps. She
jumped up in
the basket and
barked excitedly
as Zoe appeared
at the front of
the pen, beaming at her.

"Oh! Did you miss me? I really
missed you," Zoe told her, opening the
latch. "You too, yes, I missed you as well,
you great big monsters," she told Biscuit
and Choc, patting them lovingly as they
waltzed round her feet. But it was
Cookie that she sat down next to, and
Cookie she cuddled as soon as the
puppy clambered happily into her lap.

"I missed you more," Zoe whispered into her ears, as she stroked her. "I know I shouldn't really say it, but I did." She sighed. "There's some people come to look round, Cookie. Try and look like a perfect pet, won't you? You aren't old enough to go for a couple more weeks, but if they like you, they might wait."

She could hear them coming along the line of pens, now. A couple, who'd just bought a house together, and were thinking of getting a dog. They'd said they didn't mind whether it was a puppy or an older dog, but when Auntie Jo had mentioned the three gorgeous little puppies they had got excited.

"They'll be looking out for you." Zoe sighed again. "They looked nice,

I suppose. Nice-ish..." She couldn't imagine anyone being a good enough owner for her lovely Cookie. No one except her, she realized, with a miserable little gulp.

"So they decided on Jasper?" Zoe asked as she helped her aunt to clean out the food bowls, feeling a bit surprised, but very relieved. Jasper was about five years old and was a mixed-breed, mostly Labrador. He wasn't nearly as nice-looking as Cookie and her brothers, Zoe thought.

"Yes, they decided that they wanted a bigger dog after all," Auntie Jo explained. "Don't worry, Zoe. It won't be hard to find homes for those three at all. They're gorgeous. It's the older dogs that it can be hard to place."

Zoe nodded. "My friend Becca is going to get a dog soon. Becca said she'd love to come and see the puppies. She's going to ask her mum and dad if they could come this weekend. That would be OK, wouldn't it?" Her voice wobbled a little bit. "It'll only be one more week till the puppies are old enough to go to new homes then…"

Auntie Jo looked closely at her. "Yes, they'll be about seven weeks this weekend, as far as we can tell. It won't hurt them to be split up from their litter after eight weeks. It would be lovely for one of your friends to come. Zoe, are you OK, sweetheart?"

"I'll miss them, that's all," Zoe muttered.

"I know you will. Especially Cookie. You've looked after her so well. But she can't stay here, Zo, you know that. It isn't a good life for a dog, in a little pen like this, however much we love them."

"I know. But it's hard to think of someone else taking her home. I wish we could have a dog! I'd look after her so well!" Zoe burst out. Then she added quietly, "Don't worry, I know we can't..."

Auntie Jo hugged her, accidentally clanging two stainless steel dishes together behind her back, and making Zoe laugh.

"I'm so excited!" Becca raced up the steps towards Zoe, her mum following behind. She flung her arms round her. "Please can we see *all* the dogs? And the cats? I know we don't want a cat, but I'd like to see them anyway. And the guinea pigs!"

"I'll show you everything," Zoe promised, giggling. She hadn't seen her friend so hyper since her birthday party. She took them all round the shelter, saving the dog pens until last.

"You're so lucky, getting to help here all the time," Becca told her, cooing at the guinea pigs. Then she looked excitedly up at her mum. "Please can you show us the dogs now, Zoe? Mum and Dad said we might be able to get one really soon. That's what Dad's doing today – mending our garden fence so that there aren't any holes round the bottom of it, and it's safe for a dog to be in the garden. He said if we found a dog from somewhere like here, the shelter would want to come and check that we'd look after it properly."

Zoe nodded. "Yes, Auntie Jo and the other staff go and look around everyone's houses. They wouldn't let you have a cat from here if you lived on a really busy road. Or if you had small children. You'll be all right," she added. "You want a dog and it's only *really* small children that are a problem – you know, too small to understand about not pulling tails."

Becca nodded.

"Doesn't your dad want to help choose a dog?" Zoe asked curiously.

Becca's mum smiled. "This is just a first look – so we can think about what sort of dog we'd like. Becca's dad will come and see them if we tell him there's a dog we really like the look of. But he started worrying about the fence last night, and he was determined to get it done. He didn't want us to miss out on a lovely dog because the house wasn't ready."

Zoe smiled. It sounded as though Becca and her mum and dad were really serious about getting a dog. They weren't just deciding to adopt one without thinking it through, like some people did. "OK, look, well here are the dog pens. It can get a bit noisy!" she warned Becca, as several of the dogs started to bark excitedly when they realized they had visitors.

"Oh, look..." Becca whispered, glancing from side to side. "So many!

Freddie... Luca – he's gorgeous, Mum, look! He looks like a German Shepherd. Oooh! Trixie!" Becca crouched down by the little spaniel's pen. "She's so pretty..."

She glanced up worriedly at Zoe. "How do people ever choose? She's looking at me, like she really wants us to take her home, and I haven't even gone halfway along the pens yet!"

"It is hard," Zoe admitted. "If you think you really like any of the dogs, tell me, and I'll ask Auntie Jo if you can go into the pen and meet them."

"If I did that I'd never be able to say no," Becca's mum muttered. "What if we cuddled a dog and then said we didn't want him? It would be heartbreaking!"

Zoe wrinkled her nose. She supposed she was more used to the shelter than most people. "I know it's sad. But Auntie Jo and the others do find homes for all the dogs in the end. It does take a while for some of them, though." She led Becca and her mum along the row of pens. "And these..." she stopped by a pen, "are the puppies we found abandoned." She laughed as all three of them raced towards the wire of the pen. "The one with the darker brown patches is Choc and that one's Biscuit..." She pointed to the puppy with the brown eyepatch. "And this one, with the pale brown patches," she paused, "is Cookie."

"Oh, wow..." Becca murmured. "They're all so beautiful!"

"They are lovely," her mum agreed. "They look very little, Zoe. Are they old enough to be rehomed?"

"Not for about another week," Zoe explained. "But then it will be fine, although they still can't go outside for a while after that. All the dogs in here have been vaccinated, but puppies have to have a last lot of vaccinations when they're about twelve weeks old. Then they can go for walks. They'd be OK in the garden though," she added.

"You know loads about dogs," Becca said admiringly. "Please can we meet them properly? Mum, do you want to?"

Her mum nodded, smiling. "Definitely."

Zoe swallowed hard, and opened the catch on the pen. It was a good thing that Becca and her mum liked the puppies. But it was one step closer to them leaving the shelter, and Zoe.

Cookie scrabbled excitedly at the wire. Zoe had been playing with them that morning, and then she'd disappeared. Now she was back!

But there were other people too. Another girl, like Zoe, and someone else. Cookie had never seen them before. She stopped wagging her tail quite so hard, and backed up a bit as Zoe opened the door. She wasn't used to different people.

Zoe let Becca and her mum in, and Biscuit and Choc sniffed cautiously at them. Becca picked up the last bit of the rope toy, and whisked it along the ground, right in front of Choc, who quickly pounced on it, pretending to growl.

"He's so funny!" Becca giggled.

"I think he's the friendliest of the pups," Zoe told her. She looked round for Cookie, who was almost hiding behind her, watching Becca and her mum with big, anxious eyes. "It's all right, Cookie," she whispered.

Cookie pressed herself against Zoe's side, and sniffed cautiously at Becca's mum's fingers when she held them out. The new people smelled nice, but she didn't know them like she knew Zoe. She didn't mind if this lady stroked her though.

"She's very sweet," Becca's mum said. "Is this the one you bottle-fed, Zoe? You can see that she adores you."

Zoe smiled sadly. She loved it that Cookie acted like her dog, even though she wasn't. She sighed. Cookie was going to have to learn to love somebody else. Gently, she lifted Cookie up, and put her on Becca's mum's lap.

Cookie froze, and sat motionless, her shoulders all hunched up under her ears. She looked round at Zoe worriedly, but she didn't wriggle off. It was all right. Zoe was still there, very close. The lady stroked her ears, which was nice. She relaxed a little, and licked her hand.

"She's a tiny bit shy, but she's very loving," Zoe said, trying not to mind someone else cuddling Cookie. She took a deep breath. "She'd be a brilliant pet. Any of them would."

Cookie watched sadly, her ears flattening back, as they all got up. They were going, she could tell. She missed Zoe so much now that she didn't stay all day the way she used to. Zoe had been here for longer today, but Cookie still hadn't had her tea. Cookie liked it when Zoe brought her food, and sat with her while she ate. She always ate more when Zoe was there, because Zoe liked to see her eat, and she would tell her what a good dog she was, eating so nicely.

As Zoe was shutting the front of the pen, Cookie raced after her, scrabbling her claws against the wire netting and whining sadly.

"It's OK," Zoe whispered to her. "I'll be back tomorrow. I promise."

Cookie didn't know what that meant, but she understood Zoe's comforting voice. She stopped whining, and just stood up against the wire, staring after the girls as they walked down the passageway between the pens. She watched until the doors swung shut, and she couldn't see Zoe any more. Then she dropped down, and sadly padded over to their basket, her claws clicking against the worn lino on the floor.

Chapter Six

"Mum says we can make pancakes for after tea," Becca told Zoe happily, as they took their coats off.

"I love pancakes," Zoe said, trying to sound a bit more cheerful than she felt. It was a treat to go to Becca's house, but she would have preferred to have stayed at the shelter with Cookie and the others for a bit longer. It would be rude to say that, though.

The girls curled up on the sofa and watched a film. Zoe was careful not to let herself think about how nice it would be if there were a little puppy snuggled up between them watching as well. But then, next time there might be. Becca's dad was still outside fixing the fence. When they'd got back, he'd shown them the shiny new wire neatly running round the base of the old wooden fence. They'd taken him out a cup of tea, and a plate of biscuits, and he'd said gratefully that he thought he was nearly finished. It looked like their whole family was really committed to having a dog.

Becca had gone to get them both some juice, leaving Zoe watching the film – they'd both seen it before – and now she came running back in.

"Zoe! I've just been talking to Mum and Dad, and guess what!"

Zoe blinked at her in surprise.

"We're going to ask your aunt if we can reserve one of the three puppies! Mum's ringing her now! She's arranging for them to come and do a home visit too!" Becca was dancing round the room in delight, and Zoe stared at her.

This was good news. One of the puppies was going to have a brilliant home, and be beautifully looked after. Zoe would even be able to keep on seeing whichever puppy they chose. She'd know what the puppies would look like when they were grown up, after all!

But what if they chose Cookie? the voice inside Zoe's head niggled. Then Cookie would belong to someone else. She stopped herself. This was her best friend, Becca, they were talking about. Cookie would have a brilliant home.

"That's wonderful," she told Becca finally, swallowing back the lump in her throat. "Auntie Jo will be really pleased."

"Oh, and Mum says tea's ready," Becca added.

Zoe nodded. That was good. After tea it would be time for her to go home, and she wouldn't have to go on trying to be happy for Becca. She knew that she ought to be, but she wasn't.

She was burningly, horribly jealous instead, and she felt terrible for it.

"We went out yesterday to that big pet shop over by the supermarket. Have you ever been there?"

Zoe shook her head.

"I hadn't either. It's enormous, and it sells everything! You'd love it, Zoe," Becca burbled happily. "Your auntie emailed Mum a long list of stuff we'll need, and we even got some things that weren't on the list, just because they were so lovely! Lots of toys! The puppies loved playing with those toys they had in their pen at the shelter, didn't they?"

Zoe nodded. "Yes," she murmured quietly, burying her head as she got her pencilcase and book out of her bag.

"And we have to make sure that our puppy has lots to do, because they might be lonely without any others to play with. Although I'll be there, of course. Zoe, are you OK?" Becca added. "You're ever so quiet."

"I'm fine." Zoe tried to sound enthusiastic. "Did you get a rope toy? They really like that old bit of rope they've got."

"Yes! A beautiful one. Much nicer than that ratty old bit they have now."

Zoe sniffed, trying not to cry. *But they like that ratty old bit of rope,* she thought to herself. *And what if Becca chooses Cookie?* Zoe stopped herself. Whichever puppy Becca chose was going to be so lucky.

I'd be a good owner too, she said to herself miserably. *I know so much about looking after dogs. I've fed those puppies, and cleaned up after them, and washed them when they got themselves covered in Weetabix…*

"Did you hear me, Zoe?" Becca nudged her gently, and Zoe jumped.

"Um, no. Sorry. What?"

"I just said that we're going to come to the shelter on Saturday, and choose the puppy, and then it can come home with us!"

"Oh!" So soon! Zoe swallowed hard. "That's great," she muttered. "Um, I really need the loo. Tell Mrs Allan, if she comes, OK?"

Zoe tried as hard as she could to be her usual self with Becca that week, but it was so, so difficult.

Becca clearly knew that something was wrong – she wasn't stupid. Zoe kept avoiding her, and nipping off to change her library book instead of chatting with Becca and their other friends at lunch time. She spent the whole of one morning break hiding in the girls' loos, after Becca started telling her about the gorgeous collars she'd seen on a pet website. They had little pawprint designs woven in to them, and space for a phone number, so that if the dog got lost it was easy for someone to call you. It had just made Zoe feel too upset. She'd had to tell Becca she felt sick when the bell went.

Zoe hated lying to her friend all of the time, but she didn't want to admit how jealous and nasty she was really feeling.

By Friday, Becca had stopped telling her about all the things they were doing to get ready for the puppy. She almost wasn't talking to Zoe at all. And at lunch she went off and played Chain-It with a group of other girls in their class, without even asking Zoe if she wanted to join in.

"See you tomorrow morning then," she told Zoe, rather awkwardly, as they got their coats on at the end of the day.

Zoe nodded. "Yes. Bye, Becca."

And that was that. No running out to the gate together. No promises to call later about homework. Becca just walked away, leaving Zoe fiddling with the zip on her jacket, and feeling totally miserable.

Kyra was waiting for her outside school as usual – the secondary school was just up the road from Zoe's, and she usually got out later than Zoe did, but Zoe had taken ages that afternoon.

"Are you all right?" she asked. "You look really down."

Zoe shrugged. "I'm sort of not talking to Becca," she admitted. "It's horrible."

"Did you have a fight?" her sister

asked sympathetically.

"No." Zoe sighed. "It's all my fault. You know the puppies at the shelter?"

Kyra laughed. "No, Zoe, it's not as if you've ever talked about them at home."

Zoe swung her schoolbag at her sister, making a face. But Kyra was always good at cheering her up. "She's going to adopt one."

Kyra smiled, and then looked confused. "But that's good, isn't it?"

"Yes," Zoe said, in a small voice. "I just wish I could too, that's all. I'm jealous... And worse than that, I'm worried that she might choose Cookie."

"Oh, Zo..." Kyra hugged her. "Look, I haven't met these puppies but I can see how much they mean to you. Why don't we stop off at the shelter, so you can show me them?"

"But you hate dogs!" Zoe stared at her.

"I don't hate them." Kyra shrugged. "I think I'm getting better. One of my friends at school has got a really cute spaniel. I even let him sit on my lap on the sofa the other day."

"Wow, Kyra! That's great!" Zoe smiled. "Of course I'll show you the puppies. You're going to love them, 'specially Cookie – she's gorgeous. I was going to ask Mum if she could take me over there later, but let's go now." She grabbed Kyra's hand, and practically towed her down the road.

"All right, all right, keep your hair on!" Kyra grinned.

It didn't take them long to walk across

the park towards Redlands and soon they were turning into the driveway.

"I've brought Kyra to see the puppies!" she told Auntie Jo, as they popped their heads round the office door.

Auntie Jo looked up from her computer. "Hi Kyra!" She grinned. "That's great news."

"Hi Auntie Jo." Kyra smiled back. "I just thought I'd like to see them. Mum said they were really cute."

"They are." Auntie Jo nodded. "I'll call your mum and tell her you're both here. I can run you home in the car if you like."

"That would be great," said Zoe. "Come on, Kyra – they're down here." Zoe grabbed Kyra's hand and pulled her down the corridor. "Don't worry.

I don't think there are any really big dogs in the shelter at the moment," she added, seeing her sister glancing cautiously into the pens.

"I just don't like it when they jump against the wire," Kyra murmured.

"Biscuit and Choc do jump up, but they're really little," Zoe promised. "Cookie won't, not till she's worked out who you are, she's a bit shy."

"OK. Oh, Zoe, are these them?" Kyra stopped in front of the puppies' pen, smiling at them delightedly. They were all asleep, for once, flopped in a sort of puppy pile in their basket. The pile heaved and wriggled every so often, and as Zoe gently undid the front of the pen, it struggled apart and turned into three hairy, whiskery brown-and-white puppies who frisked happily around Zoe's feet.

"Do you want me to bring one of the puppies out?" Zoe asked. "Then you could stroke just one – you wouldn't have them jumping about."

Kyra nodded, and Zoe picked Cookie up. Cookie nuzzled at her happily. She'd been hoping that Zoe would come soon. She looked around curiously as Zoe carried her out of the pen, leaving her two brothers behind, looking rather jealous. Cookie stared down at them, wagging her stubby little tail.

Zoe was carrying her to another girl, a taller girl with the same dark hair and eyes. Cookie looked at her with her head on one side – she looked very like Zoe. But she didn't seem to be confident with dogs the way that Zoe was. She was looking rather nervous and, as she put out her hand, she patted her very quickly, as if she thought Cookie might snap.

Curious about this girl who looked so much like her favourite person, Cookie wriggled in Zoe's arms, stretching towards the other girl.

"She likes you!" Zoe said laughing.

"Does she?" Kyra asked, sounding surprised, and rather pleased.

"Yes, she does," said Zoe. "Do you want to hold her?"

"I don't know..." Kyra looked uncertain. "OK, let me try." Kyra nodded slowly, then let Zoe put Cookie into her arms.

Cookie snuggled up against Kyra's chin, and slowly, Kyra petted her ears. The little dog closed her eyes.

"Oh, Zoe, she's gorgeous." Kyra smiled down at the puppy. "No wonder you've been spending so much time here."

"She is, isn't she?" Zoe sighed sadly. "And now I just can't bear to think of letting her go…"

Chapter Seven

Cookie scampered down the outdoor yard, chasing after the jingly ball. It was her favourite toy. She loved the noise it made, even though she didn't quite understand where the noise came from. It was definitely hers – Zoe had given it to her. It was the only toy she bothered to fight over.

Biscuit raced past her and dived on to

the ball, rolling over with it with his paws, and growling excitedly.

Cookie let out a sharp, furious bark, and jumped on top of him, scrabbling to get the ball back. Unfortunately, Biscuit was still quite a bit bigger than she was, and he wriggled and growled. Then somehow he was sitting on top of her instead, and he still had the ball, in his teeth now. He shook it backwards and forwards, still growling, so that it jingled madly.

"Stop squabbling, you two!" Zoe ran over. "Biscuit, Biscuit, look! Stretchy bone! Your best bone! Come on! Where's it going?"

Biscuit sprang up, dropping the ball, and dancing round in circles as Zoe waved the blue rubber bone. Then she flung it down the yard, and he galloped after it like a racehorse.

Cookie seized her ball gratefully, and sat down on Zoe's feet, panting.

"You really love that, don't you?" Zoe reached down and picked her up. "Look, there's a nice sunny patch there. Let's just sit and watch those two brothers of yours being mad..."

It was a beautiful warm May day, and Zoe had shorts on for the first time that year. She ought to have been feeling happy, but all she could think about was Becca. She'd be here soon. Which puppy would she choose? Zoe ran her hand gently down Cookie's back, over and over, as Cookie shook the ball gently to-and-fro, listening to the jingly noises.

"What if she chooses you, Cookie?"
Zoe whispered. "I've been trying not to
think about it. It was bad enough just
thinking about Becca having a dog, and
me not being able to have one. But what
if it's actually you that she wants to take
back with her?" She sighed, and leaned

over, resting her cheek against Cookie's wiry fur for a moment. "I suppose at least I'd still get to see you. That's if Becca ever talks to me again, the way I've been this week. I've been awful."

Cookie looked round at her for a moment, her eyes dark and sparkly. She licked Zoe's hand.

"Thank you!" Zoe grinned. "Was that to tell me you don't think I've been awful? I have, though. I was horrible, actually. I just can't tell if it would be worse to never see you again, or to see you belong to someone else! I don't know whether to hope that Becca chooses you or that she doesn't." This time Zoe heaved a massive sigh, so that Cookie turned round and stared at her. "Sorry! Did I shake you up and down?"

"Zoe!" Auntie Jo was calling her. "Becca and her mum and dad are here! They're just getting out of their car. Go and say hello. I'll bring these three in."

"Oh! OK." Zoe gently put Cookie down, and the puppy scampered off after the ball again. She walked slowly through the shelter to the reception area, where Becca and her parents were now talking to Susie, who was on the reception desk.

"You two can chat while we just fill these in," Becca's mum told them, smiling.

Becca couldn't have told her mum how grumpy Zoe had been all week, Zoe realized gratefully. "Hi..." she said to Becca.

"Hi." Becca stared at her, and then

she pulled Zoe over into the corner, as if they were going to look at photos on the wall of the dogs and cats who'd been rehomed recently. "Zoe, is there something going on?" she asked. "Are you mad with me?"

Zoe went red and looked at her feet. "No… I…" She didn't know what to say.

"You are!" Becca cried out. "You've been acting really weird all week! What is it? What have I done?"

Zoe sighed. "Nothing. Nothing at all. I know I've been funny, but it isn't your fault. It's me. I've been jealous … jealous because you were getting a dog, and I couldn't have one, not ever. We don't have anyone at home to look after a dog, and Kyra hates them anyway. I'm so sorry I've been horrible."

"Oh, Zoe." Becca gave her friend a big hug. "Why didn't you say?" she asked her, stepping back, her eyes round with surprise. "I'd have understood!"

"I suppose I just felt stupid. And mean," Zoe muttered. "And I didn't really want to talk to you about it. You were so excited…"

Becca sighed. "I didn't think about it making you sad," she admitted. "Did I go on and on?"

Zoe gave a very small giggle. "Yes. All the time."

A voice behind them interrupted the awkward moment. It was Becca's dad. "Are you girls ready?" he asked them. "I want to see these wonderful puppies you've been telling me about!"

Becca looked anxiously at Zoe, but Zoe nodded, managing to smile and look almost as though she meant it. "Come on!"

They walked down the passage to the puppies' pen. Zoe spotted Auntie Jo coming back in from the yard, with the puppies in her arms. "There they are," she told Becca's dad, pointing. "They've been playing outside."

The puppies saw them too, and started to wriggle excitedly. Auntie Jo laughed and crouched down, letting them run down the passage towards the visitors.

Cookie dashed ahead, streaking towards Zoe on her tiny little legs. Zoe was desperate to pick her up and cuddle her. But she couldn't. It was Becca's turn.

But Becca wasn't looking at Cookie, Zoe realized. She'd crouched down, and was holding out her arms. Biscuit was running straight up to her, and now he was standing up on his hind legs, his front paws on her arms, giving happy, excited little barks. He licked her cheek and jumped, as though she was the best thing he'd ever seen!

"He remembers me!" Becca cried delightedly. "I've only met him once,

but he really remembers me! Oh, Dad,
do you like him? He's called Biscuit,
he's the most gorgeous of all of them.
Please can he be ours?"

Chapter Eight

Zoe watched, smiling, as Becca hugged Biscuit. He wriggled delightedly in her arms. So it would be a stranger who would be taking Cookie home, she realized sadly. She wouldn't see her gorgeous little puppy grow up into a beautiful dog after all.

Cookie patted her paws hopefully at Zoe's leg, asking to be picked up.

She could tell that Zoe was sad, but Cookie knew that she could make her feel better. When Zoe lifted her up at last, Cookie stood up in her arms, rubbing her whiskery nose against Zoe's cheek. That always made her laugh.

"You're so lovely," Zoe murmured, but she didn't sound much happier.

Cookie watched interestedly as the girl cuddling Biscuit gave him some crunchy treats, and carefully lifted him into a sort of box, like a small pen with a wire front. She shivered a little, burying her nose in Zoe's neck. It reminded her of the box they'd all been shut up in. It felt like a very long time ago now.

Biscuit looked confused, and whined, but the girl fed him some more treats through the wire, and then the man with her picked the box up, and carried him away down the passage to the door.

Cookie gave a little whimper of surprise. They could go away? Biscuit was going with that girl, and the other two people? She didn't understand. If they were allowed out of the shelter, why didn't Zoe take her when she went? Perhaps she would! Perhaps they were all going! Cookie's tail started to flick back and forth with excitement.

"Well, that was good, wasn't it?" Auntie Jo said, sounding really pleased. "And I meant to tell you, Zoe, a really nice-sounding family called me asking about puppies, and they were

117

interested in getting a boy puppy – so that would be you, Choc." She looked down at the puppy in her arms, who'd barked when he heard his name. "Yes, you! They're going to come and see you tomorrow, aren't they, sweetie? So we're getting there."

Zoe nodded. So that would leave just Cookie. And she wouldn't be there for much longer either, Zoe was sure.

"Oh, look, there's your mum and Kyra," Auntie Jo pointed out, and she turned to open the front of the pen, and put Choc back in.

Zoe sighed, and walked towards the pen to put Cookie in too. She'd forgotten that Mum was coming to pick her up early. She wanted them to go and do some shopping – Zoe needed new school shoes. Zoe had tried arguing that Mum could just buy them for her, but Mum had said no.

Cookie twisted in her arms, struggling frantically, and whining. She wasn't going back in the pen – she wanted to stay with Zoe! Someone had already taken Biscuit away. Only Zoe could take her.

"What's the matter?" Zoe gasped, holding the puppy tightly, and backing away from the pen, as that seemed to be what was upsetting her.

"Is Cookie OK?" Mum asked worriedly. She and Kyra had just come into the passage between the pens, and now she was hurrying towards Zoe.

"She got really upset when I was trying to put her back in the pen." Zoe cuddled Cookie close against her shoulder. She could feel the little dog's sides heaving, she was shaking so badly. "Perhaps she's sad about Biscuit going?"

She wrinkled up her brow. "It's OK, Cookie. It's OK," she whispered. But then her eyes filled with tears. "I'm telling her everything's going to be all right, but it isn't," she said miserably, looking between Auntie Jo and Mum. "Biscuit's gone to a new home, and Choc will probably go too, tomorrow, and then it'll be just Cookie left. And someone will choose her really soon, and we'll never see her again."

Auntie Jo frowned. "I wonder if she does know what's happening. Some dogs really do seem to understand, far more than you'd think they could. Maybe that's why she doesn't want to go back into that pen."

"But she has to," Zoe said dismally. "What are we going to do? Do you think she'd be better if we moved her into a different pen?"

Auntie Jo glanced at Mum, and shook her head. "No, to be honest, I think it would just be better if she went back with you."

"But then it would just be harder for her to come back." Zoe blinked, not really understanding what her auntie was saying.

"Or we could keep her?" her mum said, putting an arm round Zoe's shoulders, and gently patting Cookie.

Zoe looked puzzled. "But there's no one to look after her in the daytime."

Her mum glanced at Auntie Jo. "We've been talking about that. I told your auntie I was worried about how much you were falling in love with Cookie. That you were going to be really upset when she went to her new home."

"And I said you were so good with dogs, you really deserved to have one of your own," said Auntie Jo.

"So we've come up with a plan," said her mum.

"I'm going to have her here at work with me in the day, Zoe," Auntie Jo explained. "She can have a basket under my desk, and I'll take her for a walk at lunchtime."

"And Kyra?" said Zoe, flashing her sister a look.

"I don't feel scared of Cookie," said Kyra. "She's a little sweetheart. Mum told me how much you'd bonded with Cookie – it was actually my idea we should have her. That's why I wanted to meet her last week."

"Really?" Zoe stared round at them all, her eyes like saucers. "You mean it? We can have Cookie? So – so we could take her home now?" Zoe whispered, hardly daring to hope that they'd say yes.

Auntie Jo smiled. "Well, she obviously doesn't want to go back in that pen. I can stay here and make a big fuss of poor old Choc, so he doesn't mind being on his own. And you can borrow some food bowls and things, until you can get your own."

Zoe nodded, thinking how much pocket money she had saved up, and how she was going to spend all of it at the pet shop on the little puppy. Cookie was going to have the nicest things she could find.

"You're coming home with us," she

whispered to Cookie. "You really are."

Cookie nudged Zoe's cheek with her damp black nose, and looked hopefully at the door.

"Look at them! They're having such a good time," Zoe said, laughing at the two little brown-and-white dogs – Biscuit and Cookie. Who would have thought it? They were standing at the bottom of a huge tree, right at the end of their extending leads. And they were both jumping up and down, barking themselves silly.

"I wonder if Choc likes chasing squirrels too?" Becca said thoughtfully. "Maybe we'll see him in the park one of these days."

Zoe nodded. "I bet he does. And I bet he never catches them either."

The squirrel was sitting high up in the tree now, looking down at the two dogs in disgust. They hadn't come anywhere near getting him, and he clearly wasn't very bothered. He almost looked like he was yawning.

Eventually, Cookie and Biscuit gave up on the squirrel and wandered back to Zoe and Becca.

"Cookie's catching up on him," Becca commented. "She's nearly as big as he is now. She might even end up being bigger!"

"Maybe," Zoe agreed. "They probably won't finish growing until they're about nine months. Perhaps even a year. They're four months old now, so they've got five months more growing to do, at least. You're going to be a huge dog one day, aren't you?" she told Cookie affectionately, crouching down and ruffling her ears and stroking her back.

Becca giggled. Cookie might get bigger one day, but she and Biscuit were still tiny at the moment. Not that they seemed to think they were little at all. They strutted through the park as though they thought they were the most important dogs there.

"They wouldn't fit in that box now," Zoe said suddenly, looking up at Becca.

Becca shook her head. "I still don't know how someone could have left them like that. But I'm just glad it was you and your Auntie Jo that found them."

Zoe nodded, scratching Cookie under the chin, so that she closed her eyes blissfully, and her tail thumped on the ground.

"I know. Me too."

The Puppy
Who Was
Left Behind

Chapter One

"I'm ready to go!" Anna raced into the kitchen, dragging her wheelie suitcase, with a rucksack on her back. Her Irish Setter puppy, Fred, galloped behind her. He was very confused by the suitcase, but he liked the way it rattled.

"Are you really all packed?" Mum asked, looking at Anna's bags. "That was quick. What are you taking?"

Anna peered behind her at the suitcase and laughed at Fred. He was trying to get his nose underneath to nibble at the wheels.

"Um, I can't think of anything else to pack. Gran said not to bring loads. There isn't a lot of space on the canal boat, so I've just got my jeans, some shorts and a couple of T-shirts and a sweater. But you're coming over to visit on Sunday, anyway, aren't you? So you can bring me some more clothes if I need them."

Then she gasped. "Oh, but I need to pack for Fred! I didn't think about that." She looked doubtfully at her suitcase. There was no way Fred's food and bowls were going to fit in there, let alone all his toys. And his cushion.

Her mum laughed. "I think your gran might not mind if he brought his own bag. Just not too many toys, OK?"

Anna sighed. It was going to be hard to choose which ones to take. She was always buying Fred things with her pocket money, so he had loads of toys. His favourites were definitely all the ones that squeaked – he would play with them for ages. If Anna was too busy to throw them for him to fetch, he would do it himself. He'd worked out that he could swing his toy around in his teeth and let go, then he would chase it down the hallway and fling himself at it, skidding along on the smooth wooden floor.

Perhaps she could set out a line-up for him and see which ones he chose? But then his favourite seemed to change every day.

"Come and have some breakfast," her mum suggested. "We need to set off for the boat pretty soon."

Anna put the bags in the hallway, and then returned to the kitchen, giving her mum a hug as she came in.

"Oh! That was nice, what was that for?" her mum asked, hugging her back tightly.

"I'll miss you, that's all. And Dad. I'm really looking forward to staying on the boat with Gran and Grandad, but it'll be the first time I've stayed away without you."

"You'll have a lovely time," her mum said reassuringly. "And you're only on the boat tomorrow and Saturday before we come and see you."

"I'll have Fred as well!" Anna smiled, pouring cornflakes into her bowl and reaching for the milk jug.

Fred, who had been sniffing at one of his rubber bones that had somehow managed to get itself wedged under the fridge, leaped up excitedly as he heard his name. Anna was calling him!

He darted over to the table, skidding

like he always did on the smooth floor, and hurled himself lovingly at Anna's legs.

Anna squeaked and tipped the milk. It flooded over the edge of her bowl and across the table, dripping all over Fred's feathery, dark red fur.

He looked up at her, his big dark eyes confused. Why was he all wet? What had happened? He shook himself, and drops of milk went all over the kitchen.

"Oh, Fred..." Mum and Anna groaned at the same time. It was something they said quite a lot.

"I hope he's going to be all right on the boat," Mum went on. "It's such a small space, and he isn't very good at being cooped up, is he?"

Anna looked down at her puppy, who was now licking the milky drops off his nose with a thoughtful expression. Then he gazed up at the table again, obviously wondering how to get himself some more.

"No!" Anna moved the bowl away from the edge of the table and shook her head at him sternly. Mum was right. Fred was a wide open spaces sort of dog. They'd known before they got him that Irish Setters needed lots of exercise – at least one really good long walk (or run, really) every day. Plus it was best if they had a garden to run around in.

That was partly why they'd chosen to get an Irish Setter, when they'd all talked about what sort of dog they'd like. Anna had originally thought it would be fun to have a tiny dog, like a Chihuahua. She'd imagined sneaking the puppy into her backpack and taking him to school. But her dad had pointed out that a Chihuahua probably wouldn't be able to walk very far, and what they wanted was a dog to go on brilliant walks with.

Although their house was in a town, it was right on the edge and there was a big, wild sort of park close to where they lived. Then, if they got in the car, it only took about ten minutes to drive to a huge wood that they could explore.

And the only thing that would make all their walks even better was a dog…

Anna hadn't minded not having a Chihuahua as soon as Dad had showed her the email from the lady who had the Irish Setter puppies for sale. There were photos attached and they were so gorgeous. Anna didn't think she'd ever seen an Irish Setter before and she had never imagined a dog that colour – a sort of dark, autumn-leaves red, but with such a shine to it.

In the best photo, the puppies were all asleep, squashed up together in a basket so that Anna could hardly tell where one puppy ended and another began. Random paws and ears were sticking out all over the place, and one of the puppies was nearly falling out of the basket, but was so deeply asleep that he hadn't even noticed.

When they went to see the puppies a couple of days later, Anna was sure that she could tell which one had been half out of the basket. He had the same huge, curly-haired ears. And when he had curled up in Anna's lap and stretched himself luxuriously, his paws stuck out in that same clumsy way. As Anna ran her hand over his soft head, and he yawned and snuggled deeper into her fleece, she had known that he was just the right puppy for them.

Anna looked down at Fred – he was so much bigger now. "I'll be able to take him for long walks along the towpath, won't I?" she said to Mum. "He'll love that. He might even want to swim! Irish Setters are supposed to be good in the water." She reached down and stroked his ears. "I bet you'd be a great swimmer, wouldn't you?"

Mum looked at the puppy, sipping her tea. "Actually, I'm not sure that's such a good idea. The canal banks are pretty steep at the sides – they go straight down into the water. If Fred jumps in, he might have a hard time getting out again. And the canal's deep. Fred's probably better off waiting until we go to the seaside for his first swim." She grinned at Anna. "Then he can go into the sea with you!"

"Mmmm." Anna nodded. "I hadn't thought about how he'd get out again. I hope he doesn't want to jump off the boat. But Sunny never does that, does he?"

Sunny was Gran and Grandad's black Labrador. He always went with them on their canal boat, the *Hummingbird*. He would sit in the bow or on the roof posing, with a noble expression on his face, so people on the towpath always wanted to take photos of him. He was also very, very well-trained. Anna and Mum had taken Fred to training classes, and he was pretty good, but he was a still a bit of a scatty pup compared to perfect Sunny. Anna was fairly certain that if she put a delicious plate of sausages down in front of Sunny and told him to guard it, he would stay there watching the sausages for ever, if necessary. He wouldn't even sniff at them.

Fred, on the other hand, would wolf the sausages down in seconds, but Anna didn't really mind. She did worry that when she let Fred off the lead she wasn't always sure if he'd come back again. At least, not if there was something more interesting going on – like a really nice bit of rubbish he wanted to eat first.

Dad said it was all about the voice, and Anna just had to try and sound firmer. But Anna had noticed that Fred didn't always come back first time for Dad, either.

Chapter Two

"So are you ready to get going?" Grandad asked, smiling at Anna.

Anna nodded excitedly. She was standing on the bank, ready to cast off the mooring ropes. And Grandad was at the tiller, about to start the engine. They were going to set sail at last!

Mum had had to head home after lunch and a quick cup of tea. She was an illustrator and she had a lot of work on at the moment, which was why Anna was coming to stay on the boat. She could have stayed at home, but Mum wouldn't have been able to do anything very exciting with her, and Dad was out at work every day. Anna didn't really fancy spending the time just watching TV or lounging around in the garden.

She would have loved to go off exploring with Fred, but Mum and Dad weren't happy about her being on her own. Anna had tried to argue that Fred would be with her, but it hadn't convinced them. Fred hadn't helped much, either. He'd walked in while they were talking, carrying his lead as though he were an angelic dog. But when Anna had taken it out of his mouth, the lead had fallen apart, because he'd chewed it all the way through. After that it was quite hard to claim that Fred was super-sensible and they would be fine...

Luckily, Gran and Grandad were spending the summer on their canal boat, the *Hummingbird*, and were going to be passing quite close to where Anna and her parents lived. They'd happened to ring up for one of their regular chats, and Gran had asked Anna if she was looking forward to the summer holidays.

"Sort of," Anna had told her doubtfully. "But Mum's got to work for the first bit of the holidays so she can get everything done before we go away."

"Oh yes, she did tell me that," said

Gran. "She's got a big piece of work to finish off, hasn't she?"

"Yes." Anna sighed. "It'll be nice not having to get up and go to school, but it isn't really going to feel like the holidays. Not if we can't go out and do stuff. Usually we do trips and go off on our bikes with a picnic. Mum says she'll try and arrange for me to go and see Lucy and Jenna – you know, my friends from school. But it isn't the same if we can't have them back round to our house, too."

"Mmm, I see what you mean..." Gran said thoughtfully. "Anna, I'll have to ask your mum and dad, of course, but would you like to come and stay on the boat with us for a few days? That would give your mum lots of time to get her work done and you wouldn't be stuck inside all day."

"Just me?" Anna gasped. "On the boat? Oh, I'd love it! Would we actually get to sail? I mean, we wouldn't just be moored up on the bank?"

"Of course! Your mum and dad could drop you off, and then pick you up again a few days later, somewhere further down the canal."

"Fantastic!" Anna said gleefully. "Oh… Oh, but Gran, I've just thought. What about Fred? I was planning to play with him lots in the garden. Mum's going to be so busy – she said he'd just have to make do with a couple of short walks every day. If he's just with Mum and there's no one to play with him, he'll get all naughty and jumpy and start chewing things. Well," she added honestly, remembering the lead, "I mean, he'll chew things even more than he does already."

"Yes, I'd forgotten about Fred." Gran was silent for a moment, and Anna could tell she was thinking. "I don't see why you couldn't bring him, too. You could take him for some lovely runs along the towpath. Perhaps you could race me and Grandad in the boat!"

Anna giggled. She would probably win. Canal boats were good, but they weren't really built for getting anywhere fast.

She had passed the phone over to her mum, with a pleading, hopeful look, and it had all been arranged. Mum would drop off Anna and Fred at the boat on Thursday, the first day of the holidays, and she would stay for a week.

Anna had been to visit her grandparents on the boat before, but only for the day, and they had always stayed on the mooring – more like being in a house than a boat. So she was really excited to be setting off down the canal at last.

She heard the rumble of the engine starting up. Grandad was getting ready for them to pull away from the bank! Fred nuzzled the back of her knee with his cold nose and whined. Anna had kept him on his lead – there wasn't a lot of space on the boat, and even though Fred was only five months old, he was already getting big. His long, plumy tail was just at the right height to sweep Gran's ornaments off the shelves set into the side of the saloon – the boat's little living room. Plus everyone seemed to keep falling over him, especially Grandad. He'd tripped over Fred at least twice, and then when Fred hid under the table, Grandad trod on his tail, which was sticking out.

But Anna's real worry was the water. Even though it was a beautiful day, the canal still looked freezing. And deep. Anna wasn't tempted to swim in it at all, but she had a horrible feeling that Fred might be.

When they'd first climbed into the little well deck at the front of the boat, he kept trying to lean over the side, sniffing excitedly at the water. Anna didn't quite understand what it was that smelled so good, but then she didn't think it was fun to eat slugs, either, which were another of Fred's favourites.

It didn't help that ducks kept swimming past and circling hopefully round the bow of the boat, just in case anyone fancied throwing them some bread.

The first time he saw the ducks, Fred

froze, so excited he could hardly move. Once he'd decided they were actually real and not something that he'd dreamed up, he let out three huge, ear-splitting barks and yanked as hard as he could on his lead. He scrabbled frantically at the side of the boat with his claws, trying to throw himself overboard to catch the tempting feathery things.

"Fred!" Anna gasped, clutching at his lead. "Hey, come back!"

The ducks suddenly found something interesting to go and look at close to the other bank, and Mum had grabbed hold of Fred's collar, helping Anna to haul him back.

Fred carried on growling for a bit, before he finally gave up and accepted that they'd gone.

"Wow..." Anna muttered. "I didn't think about ducks. He was almost straight in. Is there such a thing as a dog lifejacket?"

She had a lifejacket on herself – Gran had explained that they knew she wasn't silly enough to fall in, but accidents did sometimes happen and it was better to be safe.

"I'm sure you can get them. Does Sunny have a lifejacket?" Mum asked, glancing over at the black Labrador, who was sunbathing on the roof of the boat. He was asleep, or he seemed to be, but Anna noticed he had one eye half-open, as though he was keeping watch. She had a feeling he was partly watching for Fred, in case he did something awful.

Gran shook her head. "No… He's actually a very good swimmer. And he's so sensible, we've never thought we needed one."

Anna sighed. "Was Sunny sensible even when he was a puppy?"

"I think he was…" Grandad frowned, trying to remember.

Anna nodded. It made sense. She found it difficult to imagine perfectly behaved Sunny as a puppy at all!

Gran shook her head. "He certainly wasn't! Don't you remember my best pink shoes?"

Grandad laughed. "Yes! How could I forget?"

Gran sighed. "Oh, they were lovely, those shoes. I still miss them. He chewed one of them to pieces! The other shoe was still perfect and somehow that made it even worse!" She gave Anna a hug and rubbed Fred's ears. "Fred will settle down, don't worry. I don't think Irish Setters are quite as ... obedient as Labradors, but he just needs to grow up a bit."

Anna nodded gratefully, feeling a bit better. She looked up at Sunny, trying to imagine him with a pink shoe dangling out of his mouth.

Sunny snorted a little and laid his nose on his paws, as though he'd never done anything like that in his life.

Fred gave up on the ducks after that. He didn't understand why he wasn't allowed off the lead. Usually when they went out to the woods or the park, he could go racing away. He loved to run, but there wasn't a lot of running space on the boat. It was only a few paces wide, for a start. And there wasn't a hallway to race up and down like there was at home. There didn't seem to be a garden either, only the long pathway at the edge of the water.

Fred was just as unsure about the water as Anna was. He'd never seen so much of it in one place before and he definitely thought it looked cold, too. But when he'd seen the ducks, somehow he forgot to worry about that.

He peered up at Sunny, who was still snoozing on the roof. He didn't understand how Sunny could sleep through the loud rattling rumble of the engine. Perhaps he was just used to it. If Sunny would only wake up, maybe they could go running together. Fred was pretty sure he would be the fastest. He always was.

Sunny was watching him, Fred

realized. This was his boat, Fred could smell that it was. He huffed and turned round on Anna's feet so that he wasn't looking at the bigger dog any more.

He was starting to wish they were back home.

Chapter Three

By the end of the day, Fred seemed to settle down to being on the boat. Anna had brought along his big cushion to make him feel more at home. Fred leaped on to it gratefully when Anna put it out next to her bed.

Anna had been a bit confused as to where she would actually sleep when Gran had invited her to stay on the boat, because she could only remember there being one double bedroom. She'd thought she might have to sleep in her sleeping bag on the floor somewhere, but Gran had laughed and promised her a proper bed.

That evening she explained that boats were all about saving space, and showed Anna how the table in the kitchen area folded down and the benches on either side of it slid round to make a comfy little bed. It was very clever. And it meant that Anna and Fred drifted off to sleep that night with Gran and Grandad sitting in their armchairs, watching television, but with the sound turned down so low that it mixed with the soft lapping of the water against the hull.

Anna dreamed of floating off across the water in a tiny bed.

On Friday everyone woke up early. Anna did as Gran suggested and took Fred for two lovely long runs, racing the boat. They could run just as fast as the *Hummingbird*, as the part of the canal they were on had a five-mile-an-hour speed limit, which was a good sort of speed to keep up.

Anna could tell that Fred was feeling better after all that exercise. By the time they stopped at one of the locks late that afternoon, and Anna helped Grandad open the lock gates, he was slumped in the long grass, panting happily. Anna had to coax him up and on to the boat. Then he made straight for his big cushion, flopping down on to it.

Anna laughed. Fred still slept the way he had when he was a puppy, all legs sticking out everywhere. It did mean he took up a lot of room inside the boat. They kept having to step round him. But he was very sweet and he wasn't being naughty, so no one minded.

Anna did wish that Fred got on better with Sunny, though. Actually, it didn't really seem to be Fred's fault. He was always very friendly with other dogs, even smaller ones, and he loved to chase and play and romp up and down the park with them. He even had a couple of "best friends" – a spaniel called Lottie and a tiny Jack Russell called Max, who bossed Fred and Lottie around all the time.

Anna had thought that Fred and Sunny would probably get on in the same sort of way. She'd even imagined that it would be a nice treat for Sunny to have another dog for company.

Unfortunately, Sunny didn't seem to see it that way. He'd never shared his house or his boat with another dog, and he didn't see why he had to start now. Especially with a dog like this, who frisked around everywhere the whole time, and kept sniffing at him and creeping up on him and yapping excitedly. Sunny didn't like it at all and he snapped when Fred nuzzled at him, and let out a furious growl when the pup jumped into his basket. Fred jumped out again quickly, creeping away with his head hanging low and his back rounded in a shamed sort of crouch.

Fred was confused. He wasn't used to sharing his home either, but the other dogs in the park liked him to play. He was only doing what he always did.

Still, at least he had Anna. He'd dragged his cushion right up to her strange little bed on the first night, so that he could curl up close to her. In fact, that was one thing that was better than home – there he slept in the kitchen. Now he was close enough to hear her breathing, and for her to reach down a hand and stroke him sleepily.

The two long walks meant that Fred fell asleep early that night, curled up on Anna's feet as they ate dinner. He only really woke up long enough for a last quick trip out on to the towpath before Anna went to bed.

Fred woke up early Saturday morning, feeling full of energy. At home he would have scratched hopefully at the back door until someone let him out into the garden, or raced madly up and down the hallway, chasing his toys. But there just wasn't enough room for that here.

He gnawed fiercely at one of his rubber bones for a while – it was easy to find, as he discovered he'd been asleep on top of it. It wasn't as good as a walk, though. He sat up and stared hopefully at Anna, who was still sleeping. He put his paws up on the edge of the bed and whined, but she only made a strange sleepy noise and rolled over away from him.

Fred slumped back on to his cushion, and looked at Sunny, who was curled up in his basket on the other side of the saloon. Maybe Sunny would play? There wasn't a lot of room, but perhaps they could chase each other up and down?

He uncurled himself and crept over to Sunny's basket, whining a little.

Sunny woke up and stared grumpily at him, but Fred just thumped his huge feathery tail on the boards and put his head on one side, his ears twitching with excitement. Then he dropped down in front of the basket, stretching his paws out, and let out a few sharp yaps.

Sunny sat up and glared at him, and let out a furious growl.

Fred wriggled backwards, upset and a bit frightened. Why wouldn't Sunny play with him? He barked, suddenly and loudly, so that Anna woke up with a start and banged her head on a shelf. She yelped, rubbing the back of her head.

Fred panicked completely. Sunny was growling at him, and now Anna sounded upset, and he didn't understand what was going on. He ran backwards and forwards across the boat, barking and bumping into the shelves along the walls, and then the little folding table where Gran always put her tea.

The table went flying and banged against Fred's front leg. He whimpered and came to a stop. He crouched in the middle of the cabin, his paw held up miserably.

"What's going on?" Grandad came out of the bedroom, looking rumpled and sleepy and cross. "Is somebody hurt? What have you done, you silly dog!"

Fred whimpered again and wriggled backwards behind one of the armchairs. Grandad's voice was low and rumbly, and not like any of the voices that Fred was used to. He could tell that the deep-voiced person was very cross, and Anna was crying, and Sunny was still letting out low, furious growls. Now everyone was angry with him...

Chapter Four

"What on earth happened?" Gran asked, hurrying out of the bedroom and putting an arm around Anna. "Did you bump yourself, Anna? And where's Fred?"

"Over there," Anna sniffed, still rubbing her head. "Behind the armchair. I think he's hurt his paw – the table fell on it."

"Oh dear," Gran murmured. "Well, thank goodness there wasn't anything on it. It's lucky I moved that little vase yesterday. If that had smashed, he could have cut himself."

Grandad went over to pick up the table. "Not broken. It's fine. Come on out, Fred." He crouched down and looked round the armchair, but Fred had crept right behind it now. All that they could see was a dark pinkish nose and they could hear him whimpering. "Poor old boy. He's really scared." He sighed. "Sorry, Anna, that's probably my fault. I shouted and he doesn't really know me."

Anna slid down from the bed and hurried over to Fred's hiding place. "Hey, Fred. It's OK. Come on out."

Fred sniffed cautiously at Anna's outstretched hand and slowly, gradually, he wriggled out from behind the chair. But he was shivering and he still looked miserable. Anna carefully checked his paw, but it wasn't bleeding and it didn't seem to be hurting him any more.

"Oh dear." Gran sighed. "Was it another squabble with him and Sunny, do you think?"

"That's what it sounded like," Grandad agreed. "Lots of barking and scuffling. I suppose Sunny thinks it's his boat. He's never had another dog on board before. And he isn't used to a friendly puppy like Fred, all bounce and tail-wagging."

"What are we going to do?" Anna whispered. Grandad had picked up the table, but there were still newspapers everywhere and Fred had knocked over a pile of books. A couple of Gran's pretty china animals were on the floor, too, and Anna really hoped they hadn't been broken. The room was a mess.

Gran frowned. "I'm not sure. They really aren't getting on, are they? I know Fred's only trying to be friendly, but he's just got so much energy. He isn't the right sort of dog to be squashed up on a boat." She shook her head, worriedly. "I'm sorry, Anna, I didn't think about this properly. I was just so excited about you coming to stay with us."

Anna nodded and sniffed. "Do we have to go home?" she whispered. She didn't want to, but it wasn't fair on Gran and Grandad to have Fred spoiling their beautiful boat.

"I don't think it's that bad..." Gran murmured. "Let's all get dressed and have some breakfast. If you throw some clothes on quickly, you could take Fred for a quick walk, maybe? That'll cheer him up and burn off some of his energy. And your grandad and I can think about what to do."

Fred wagged his tail a little as he saw Anna pick up his lead. A walk. It was all he had wanted, really, but everything seemed to have gone wrong.

Still, as he hopped carefully over on to the bank and sniffed the cool morning air, everything seemed better. The grass was lovely and wet under his paws, and interesting things had been running along the towpath in the night – rabbits and those hard-to-catch ducks. He sniffed busily, nuzzling into the clumps of grass and under the brambly hedges.

"Come on, Fred," Anna said at last, yawning. "We should go back now. Don't you want your breakfast? I'm starving."

All the same, she walked slowly as they turned back towards the boat, letting Fred rootle around in the long grass. There were scuffling noises in the hedges and indignant twitterings. She smiled. "Watch it, Fred. You'll get your nose pecked in a minute, mister."

Even though Fred didn't like being shut up and he kept getting in trouble with Sunny, Anna loved being out here with him. She didn't want to go home.

But she couldn't see what else they could do.

"So, your mum and dad are coming over for lunch tomorrow," Grandad said, buttering his toast.

"Mmm…" Anna nodded. And they were going to say that she and Fred should go back home with them, she just knew it. She sighed.

"We were thinking perhaps they could take Fred home, too," Gran said.

Anna stared at her. "Just Fred? And leave me here?"

Gran and Grandad both nodded, and Anna glanced from one to the other, confused.

"But what about Mum? She won't be able to look after him properly. That's why I had to bring him. I mean, I wanted to, anyway, but it was mostly because he needs someone around."

Anna sniffed and shook her head apologetically. "I know he made a real mess of the boat, but if he didn't get walked enough at home, he'd probably do the same. He chews things when he's bored. If I'm home at least I can play with him in the garden."

"Ah, but you see, your mum's got loads of work done already," Gran explained. "She called me while you were on your walk with Fred. She said she was glad to hear you were having a lovely time on the boat and she didn't have to worry about you. I'm sure she'd be able to fit in walking Fred now she's got a bit more time."

"Oh..." Anna frowned to herself. If they both went back, her mum would be worrying about whether

Anna was all right, stuck at home while she was trying to work. "I suppose you're right," she murmured. She really didn't want Fred to go, but it did seem like the best solution. If you didn't count how much she would miss him.

Anna took Fred for another really long walk along the towpath that morning. Partly because she knew she was going to miss him so much after he went home tomorrow, but also because she was hoping, just a little bit, that if she wore him out enough, he'd be really good. Then maybe Gran and Grandad would change their minds and say it was OK for him to stay.

They moored up that afternoon next to a break in the woods that ran along one bank of the canal. The dark trees opened out and there was a huge field, dotted with big, old oak trees. Anna looked out at it delightedly. She couldn't wait to explore, and Fred's tail was wafting back and forth excitedly as he looked at all that open space to run in.

"It's beautiful!" Anna said to Grandad, as she helped him tie the boat up to the mooring posts on the bank. Fred was pulling hopefully at his lead, as though he wanted to go for a walk right now.

"Isn't it?" Grandad agreed. "I'm glad we were able to get this far before your mum and dad come to see us. This is a great spot – it's not too far from the road, though you'd never guess it, and there's a café with space to park cars over on the other side of that field. It's a popular mooring spot, so we're not allowed to stay here too long."

"You mean like you have to move on from parking spaces?" Anna asked, surprised. She hadn't realized it worked the same way for boats.

"Mm-hm. We can stay until Monday morning, but that's all."

Anna giggled. "It's not like the end of our road where you can only park for two hours, then!"

Grandad snorted. "Well, not quite."

"So – Mum and Dad will walk across here tomorrow, to come and see us?" Anna asked, with a tiny sigh.

"Yes. Are you OK, Anna?" Grandad looked at her worriedly. "I know you'll miss Fred, but he really will be happier back home, I think."

"Maybe," Anna agreed quietly. She couldn't help thinking that Fred would be happiest wherever she was. He was used to her being around, except when she was at school. And even then he would be at the front door to meet her as soon as she got back, flinging himself at her, barking and whining as if he'd thought he was never going to see her again.

Grandad gave her a sympathetic smile. "Look, why don't you take him for a really good run across that field now? Your gran's going to be a while cooking the dinner. You might even be able to let him off the lead – there doesn't seem to be anyone else around. Just don't go out of the field, though, will you? So that I know where you are?"

Anna nodded. "I promise. Come on, Fred!"

Fred looked over at the field hopefully, and his long tail swished slowly from side to side.

"Yes! Walk! Come on!" Anna patted her hand against her leg, and Fred leaped joyfully forward, prancing through the gate into the field. It was long, tussocky grass, and he and Anna raced across it, Anna laughing and stumbling as she tried to keep up with him.

"Slow down a minute! Fred, come on, stop. Then I can get your lead off. Yes, you see, silly, that's what you want, isn't it?" Fred danced about excitedly while Anna unclipped the lead, and then he bounded away, barking like a mad thing.

Anna watched him, giggling. She loved it when he ran so fast that his ears flapped. Today, he looked as though he might even take off.

Then she sighed and wrapped her arms around her middle. She knew that sending Fred home tomorrow was the sensible thing to do, but she still wasn't happy about it. And she didn't think Fred would be, either.

Chapter Five

Anna's mum and dad arrived the next day in time for lunch. They'd brought a lovely picnic with them, with loads of sandwiches and a chocolate cake, and they ate it under one of the oak trees in the big field. Then Dad and Anna played Frisbee with Fred, sending him racing across the field. Fred was excellent at catching the Frisbee – he did huge ballet-dancer leaps to grab it. But as the afternoon wore on, Anna kept thinking that Mum and Dad would have to go soon, and take Fred with them. She hardly ate any of the lasagne that Gran had made for dinner. Somehow she just didn't feel hungry.

"We should get back," Anna's dad said at last, peering at his watch. "We've got work tomorrow and it must be nearly your bedtime, Anna, even if it is the holidays. It's starting to get dark. But it's been a really good day."

Anna gulped and looked over at Fred, who was snoozing in the corner. He looked angelic – maybe Gran would say he could stay after all? But then she blew her hot fringe off her forehead, and remembered that it was so warm because the saloon doors were tightly closed. Closed to keep Fred in, so he didn't try to leap over the side of the boat. He'd nearly jumped into the canal again this morning, after he'd spotted a swan sailing grandly past.

"Do you want to gather Fred's stuff together?" Mum suggested gently. Then she saw Anna's worried face. "It'll be OK," she said. "I've got so much work done over the last few days, I can definitely take time off for some really good walks with Fred."

"I know," Anna murmured, picking up Fred's bowls and tipping his water into the kitchen sink. She polished them dry with some kitchen roll and started to fill the bag with all of Fred's things. One of the rubber bones squeaked as she picked it up, and Fred bounced up off his cushion, as though Anna had shouted his name.

He trotted over to her happily, waiting for her to throw him the toy. It was going to be difficult playing catch, with all these people squashed on to the boat, but it would still be fun.

But Anna just stared down at him sadly and put the squeaky bone into the bag that they'd brought with them to the boat. Fred watched her, confused, and then realized what this meant. Of course! They were going home! He wagged his tail so hard it thumped against Anna's legs, but for some reason she didn't look very happy.

Helpfully, he hurried back to his cushion and picked it up in his teeth, ready to go.

Dad laughed. "Look, Fred's keen to get in the car." He came over to Anna, and hugged her. "Don't worry, he'll be fine. I can take him for a walk after work, too, you know."

"I just think he'll miss me," Anna sniffed. Or maybe he wouldn't at all, and that would be almost worse.

Dad gave her a kiss and gathered up the bag, and Mum clipped on Fred's lead.

Anna and Gran and Grandad came out to the bow of the boat to wave goodbye, and even Sunny got up out of his basket to come and see what was going on.

Mum and Dad jumped over on to the bank, and Fred did a giant leap after them. He didn't look too worried, Anna thought sadly.

But then as Mum went to open the gate, Fred looked back and realized that Anna wasn't coming with them. He let out a little whine of surprise and stopped to wait for her.

"Come on, Fred!" Mum pulled gently on his lead, but Fred was pretty heavy when he didn't want to move.

"Oh..." Anna whispered. "He wants to stay."

She'd been wrong to think she'd be upset if he just walked away. It was much worse watching Fred turn his head from side to side, glancing anxiously between her and Mum and Dad, obviously not understanding what was going on. She wouldn't have minded if he'd trotted happily across the field, after all. She wished he had.

Mum pulled the lead a bit harder, and Fred lurched to his feet, padding unwillingly after her.

Anna started to cry, and Gran

hugged her. Even Sunny came over to her and pressed comfortingly against her leg. She turned her face into Gran's chest so she didn't have to watch.

Fred could hear Anna crying as Mum pulled him across the field and he hated it. He knew that was a bad noise – that it meant something was wrong. He didn't want Anna to sound like that, and he stopped suddenly, yanking at his lead so hard that he slipped his collar. He pulled even harder, dragging it over his ears, and then he was free.

Anna's mum had been holding the lead tightly, but when Fred got free she lost her balance and half fell over. "Fred, no! Come back! Bad dog!"

Fred flattened his ears and looked at

her worriedly. He'd done something wrong, he knew he had. But it couldn't really be wrong, because he needed to go and help Anna. He laid his ears back apologetically, and then he turned and raced back across the field to get to her.

"Fred, get back here!" Anna's dad yelled, dropping the bags and starting to chase after him. "No! Here!"

Fred flinched as he heard the shouting. He hated it when people shouted at him, and it seemed to have been happening all the time recently. Anna's grandad kept being cross with him, and now Dad was as well. He darted through the gate and saw Anna, still standing on the boat, watching sadly.

"Fred!" She leaned towards him, but Grandad was there, too, looking annoyed – and Sunny.

Sunny barked at him and Fred stopped, looking uncertainly at Anna. Then he heard Dad pounding up behind him and he skittered sideways along the path, not sure what to do. As Dad reached out to grab at him, he shot away up the towpath, and darted under the fence and into the shadows of the wood.

"What happened?" Anna gasped. "Fred was off his lead, Dad!"

Her dad nodded grimly. "He slipped his collar."

Mum hurried up to the gate. "You were right, Anna. He was upset about going without you."

Dad sighed. "I'll go and get him. Naughty thing!"

"Shall I come, too?" Anna suggested, putting her foot up on the side of the boat, ready to jump over to the bank.

Dad shook his head. "Better not. He's in a bit of a tizzy, isn't he? I don't want him getting any more excited."

Anna watched anxiously as Dad headed into the woods. Poor Fred. He really wouldn't understand what was happening. He was probably hiding under a bush somewhere, feeling even more miserable than she was.

Anna wriggled free of Gran's arms, and jumped out on to the bank. "I know Dad said to wait here, but I can't!" she told Mum. "I won't go into to the wood. I just want to see if Dad's found him yet."

She was pretty sure that he hadn't. She could hear him calling for Fred, and he was sounding more and more worried every time. Anna shivered as she came into the shadows of the trees hanging over the fence. It was getting late, after nine now, and the sun had set. It was almost dark.

A sudden, horrible thought made her stop, just as she was about to lean over the fence and peer in to look for Dad and Fred.

What if they didn't find him?

It was even darker in the wood, and Fred's red coat would blend into the shadows. If he was upset and hiding, Dad just wouldn't see him.

Anna gasped and climbed up on to the fence, trying to see through the dark trees.

"Anna!" Mum called. "Don't climb over there."

Anna twisted round to look at her. "Can't I go and help look? Please? Fred will come if I call him, Mum. He's scared, but he isn't scared of me."

"No, wait there." Mum dropped the bags and came over to her. "Dad will find him. He'll be back in a minute with Fred, I'm sure he will."

But just then, Dad came hurrying back up the thin thread of a path, a worried expression on his face. "I can't find him," he said anxiously. "The silly dog's gone racing off somewhere. I'm sorry, but I think we should all go and look and call for him. Have you got a torch?" he shouted across to Gran and Grandad.

Grandad nodded and went back into the boat. He returned with two big torches and handed one to Dad.

"My phone works as a torch as well," Mum said. "We'd better split up, then we can look everywhere. Anna, come with me, OK?"

Anna nodded. She was too upset to say anything. Her beautiful Fred was lost, hiding somewhere in this horrible wood, all alone.

Fred huddled in a hole under the roots of a tree, watching the trees get darker and darker in front of him. He wasn't exactly sure where he was, but he thought he could find his way back to the boat. He'd gone quite far, racing as fast as he could away from Sunny and all the angry people shouting at him. But he could always follow his own scent back the way he'd run.

He just wasn't sure that he wanted to go back. Not yet, anyway. Dad had been trying to take him away from Anna, and he didn't understand why.

Fred snuffled at the dusty leaf litter in the bottom of his hiding place. What else could he do? He didn't want to stay here. It was getting dark and even though he could see quite well in the dim light, he didn't like it much. He wanted to be sitting on his comfortable cushion, with Anna stroking his ears.

Fred's ears twitched. There were footsteps coming down the path. He wriggled uncertainly and poked his nose out of the hole. Someone was calling for him! Fred was about to jump out and see who it was when he recognized the voice. It was Grandad, sounding worried and calling, "Here, Fred! Fred! Come on, boy!"

Fred listened and then he scrunched back up into his hiding place, making himself small. Grandad had been cross with him back on the boat, and Fred could hear the strain in his voice now, too.

He wouldn't go back just yet. Not while people were still cross. He'd stay hidden a little while longer.

Chapter Six

"But we can't stop looking!" Anna stared up at them all in horror.

"It's too dark," Dad explained. "We can hardly see, even with the torches, sweetheart."

"Someone could trip over. If you put your foot in a rabbit hole you could break an ankle," Mum added, putting her hands on Anna's shoulders"I know you want to find Fred, and I'm really sorry. But we just aren't going to find him like this," said Gran.

Anna shook her head, looking back out at the dark trees. "We can't leave him out there all night. He'll be scared!" She took the torch out of Dad's hand, and started to flash it around the path again, calling for Fred. Her voice sounded hoarse and her throat hurt, she'd been shouting for so long. "There's a noise!" she gasped, starting forward excitedly. "A rustling, can't you hear it? It has to be Fred!"

But when the creature came out from between the trees, it stopped in surprise, instead of running to greet them. Anna's torch flashed on to a pair of frightened, glowing eyes. She rushed to hug it, but the fox whisked away, its red bushy tail nothing like Fred's beautiful feathers.

"It wasn't him," Anna whispered miserably.

"It was only a fox," Gran nodded, as Anna sagged with disappointment, her shoulders drooping. "Anna, it's so late, you're exhausted. We've been searching for two hours now. You need to go to bed. We all do. Your mum and dad have still got to drive back."

"But Fred..."

"I think he's upset and he's hiding," Dad explained, hugging her. "We can start looking again tomorrow. We'll get up really early and come straight here. I'll just have to go into work late. Fred's not used to the dark, is he? When it's light he'll feel better and come out. He'll want to come back to us then."

"I want him back now!" Anna sobbed.

She hated the thought of Fred being too scared to come and find her.

"We all do," Dad said, but Anna couldn't help thinking he was only saying that. If he really wanted Fred back, they'd keep looking all night.

"Just one more look," she begged, pulling away. Then her feet seemed to wobble underneath her and everything went blurry. Someone grabbed her and she heard Mum's voice. It seemed to be coming from a long way away.

"Anna, you're asleep on your feet! Come on."

Anna lay in her little bed, worrying. Even though she'd been almost asleep out in the wood, now she felt horribly awake. She kept putting her hand out to stroke Fred to make her feel better, and then she'd realize all over again that he wasn't there.

The boat rocked a little, and she sat up, looking hopefully at the door. "Did you find him?" she gasped, as Gran and Grandad came in. She had been so upset when they took her back to the boat that Grandad had promised to go and have one last look if she would be sensible and get into bed.

"No, Anna, I'm sorry," said Grandad. "But I was thinking – Irish Setters are good trackers, they were bred for hunting. I'm pretty sure Fred will find his own way back. We'll probably see him sitting in the front of the boat, watching the ducks in the morning!"

"Or he'll wake us up at four o'clock scratching at the door," Gran put in, perching on the end of Anna's bed.

"You really think so?" Anna sniffed.

Gran hesitated, just for a second, but Anna had felt it.

"What I think is that you need to get to sleep," Gran said quickly. "If we do have to go looking for Fred tomorrow morning, you'll want to be up early. We're going to bed now, too."

Anna listened to them fussing around getting ready for bed, and gradually everything grew quiet. But she still couldn't sleep. If only Sunny and Fred had got on better, this would never have happened. But now poor Fred had been driven away.

Everyone had tried to tell her that it would be fine – that Fred would be back soon, or that they'd at least find him tomorrow morning. Anna wanted so much to believe that they were right, but she couldn't help thinking about what might happen if they weren't.

Where was Fred? What if he'd run all the way through the wood to the road? Mum and Anna had been through the wood and seen the cars roaring past…

Anna shivered. Surely Fred wouldn't

have gone out into the road, would he? He was used to walking in town, and they'd been careful to train him to stop and sit at the edge of the pavement. But what if he didn't see what it was in the dark? It was a country road, with a grassy verge and no kerb. He might not realize it was a road at all.

Anna rolled over and buried her face in the pillow to try to stop herself crying. But she couldn't hold back the tears seeping out of the corners of her eyes.

Fred could get run over. What would she do if she never saw him again?

Fred stuck his muzzle out of the gap under the tree roots and sniffed cautiously. He'd never been out this late before. He wriggled out of his hiding place and shook himself. His legs felt strange, cramped up and wobbly. He walked slowly around in a little circle, sniffing for the scent trail back to the boat. He was jittery and upset, and it seemed harder to find a scent than it usually was. But at last he found it and began to trot back through the wood.

He wriggled under the fence and came back out on to the canal bank. He could see the boat, looming up out of the canal like a darker patch of shadow. Fred slunk across the grass towards it, not sure what to do. The boat was quiet and all the lights were out. Everyone was asleep, perhaps. They might shout at him again if he woke them up. He went up closer, standing on the edge of the bank, his ears twitching as he tried to listen for Anna.

Quietly, carefully, he jumped into the deck well at the bow of the boat. He could stay here till the morning, he thought. And Anna would see him when she woke up. But then he heard a shifting, creaking noise from inside, and paws padded over towards the door.

He had forgotten about Sunny.

There was a low, uncertain growl from the other side of the door and Fred backed away miserably, bumping up against the side of the boat.

He jumped back on to the bank, his paws scrabbling a little against the damp, slippery grass, and padded away. He needed Anna, but he couldn't get to her without going past Sunny first. He would have to wait until morning, he decided wearily. All of him ached after the hours curled up in that uncomfortable hole. And he was so tired.

Fred wandered along the bank, sniffing at the other two boats on the mooring. He couldn't smell any dogs on either of them. Cautiously, he put his paws up on the side of the hull of the last boat and looked in at the stern well. There was a canvas awning folded up, and he jumped lightly down into the boat, wriggling under it and curling up, fidgeting to settle his aching paws.

Then, at last, he fell asleep.

Chapter Seven

Anna had strange, horrible dreams all night. She and Sunny and Fred went round and round in circles, chasing each other, and however hard Anna ran, she seemed to be standing still. In the worst dream, which seemed to keep coming back, she and Fred both had wings, and Anna was flapping and flapping and trying to catch up with him, but he was always too fast.

She woke up with a jolt, gasping for breath. The dream seemed so real that she expected her arms to ache. She stretched them out gingerly, but they felt just like they usually did.

"You're awake, Anna!" Gran bustled over to her. "I was about to get you up."

Anna blinked and then looked around, her fingers clenching on her bedcover. "He's not back, is he?" she asked, her voice very small. She knew he wasn't. He'd have been all over her by now, barking and licking.

Gran sighed. "No. No, he isn't yet."

"What time is it?" Anna asked, jumping out of bed and starting to pull on her clothes. It didn't look like early morning – the sun was bright already, and Gran was dressed and making breakfast.

"It's eight o'clock. Oh, I know you wanted to wake up early, Anna, but you were so tired, and you were up so late last night."

Anna stared at her in horror. How could they have let her sleep for so long? "I have to go out and look for Fred!" she gasped, hopping her way into her jeans.

"Grandad's been out for a while, searching the wood again," her gran explained. "And your mum and dad will be here soon to help as well. They said they'd just go and walk along the road that runs by the back of the wood first."

Anna nodded miserably. So it wasn't just her worrying that Fred had gone further than the wood.

"We'll have to move the boat this morning as well," her gran said gently.

Anna yanked her sweater over her head and turned to look at Gran in horror. She'd forgotten that they couldn't stay on the mooring. "We've still got to go?" she whispered. "We have to leave Fred behind?"

"We won't go far, I promise. Just a little further up the canal. Grandad says he's sure there's somewhere we can stop and moor up, about a mile further on from here. Then we'll hurry back."

Anna nodded, but she felt like howling. Somehow it seemed like giving up on Fred, even though she knew they were coming back.

The boat shook a little as Grandad stepped back on board, and he came in through the saloon door.

Anna opened her mouth to ask, but Grandad shook his head. "No sign at the moment, Anna, sorry. But your mum called, saying they've parked over where they were last night. They're going to walk along to the village and go into the shops to ask if anyone's seen him." He eyed Anna anxiously and added, "They printed out a few posters, too."

"But Fred's only been gone one night…" Anna said, shaking her head. "He's not really lost, is he? We don't need posters up!" Putting up posters made it feel all the more real.

Grandad shook his head. "I know what you mean, but if someone sees Fred and doesn't realize he's lost – if they just think he's off the lead and they can't see his owner, they won't do anything, will they? People will know to be looking out for him if they see a poster."

"I suppose so," Anna murmured. She was glad Mum and Dad hadn't come to the boat before they set off with the posters. She was pretty sure that a LOST poster with Fred's photo on it would have turned her into a wobbly, crying mess. And she'd be no use to Fred like that. She shook herself briskly and sniffed.

"If I take a piece of toast with me, can I go and look for him now? Just one more quick look before we have to move the boat? Please? I'll be back soon."

Gran and Grandad exchanged glances, but then Gran said, "If you're careful. Stay on the path, Anna, though, won't you?"

Anna nodded eagerly, snatching up the toast and heading for the door. Sunny thumped his tail against his basket as she went past, and Anna stopped to pat him quickly. She'd felt furious with him last night, while she was lying there worrying about Fred. But it wasn't really his fault. He just liked things his own way, nice and quiet, without a big, bouncy puppy jumping all over him.

She leaped from the boat to the towpath, and headed back into the wood. It looked so different this morning, with sunlight pouring in through the gaps in the trees. It wasn't the eerie, almost frightening place it had been the night before. There were birds singing, and as Anna hurried down the path, a tiny rabbit suddenly turned tail and disappeared into the bracken.

Anna's mouth twitched into half a smile. Even though she felt awful, the rabbit's surprised expression had been so funny. Then she stopped and looked around thoughtfully. Fred would have chased that rabbit, if he'd seen it. He would have jumped after it, barking so loudly that the rabbit and all of its friends and relations would be hiding in their burrows in seconds. That rabbit hopping calmly around on the path made Anna think that Fred wasn't anywhere near.

She gulped and swallowed. Maybe he was long gone, then. Maybe he had gone out on to the road, and Mum and Dad had the right idea to go there first.

Anna turned and headed back to the boat. Maybe if Mum and Dad weren't too far away, she could go and find them and help them look while Gran and Grandad moved the *Hummingbird*. She couldn't bear the thought of going further away and wasting all that time.

"Hello!" Grandad waved to her from the towpath as she came out of the trees. "I'm just going to walk up and ask the people on the other boats to watch out for Fred. Do you want to come?"

Anna nodded. She didn't want to, actually. She hated the thought of telling people that Fred was lost. Like the posters, it made it seem as though he really was. But she'd do anything to get him back, she told herself.

The people on the next boat were sitting on their bow deck, drinking tea, so it was easy to talk to them.

Anna liked that about being out on the canal – everyone seemed very friendly. Even when someone had made a mistake and messed up going into a lock, people would always come and help instead of getting annoyed.

"What, your lovely Irish Setter?" the lady asked, as Grandad explained.

"Yes," said Grandad. "We're especially worried as we've got to move on from the mooring this morning. We're going to stop a little bit further on and walk back, but just in case we miss him, it would be great if you could keep an eye out. Here's our mobile number."

"Of course we'll look out for him," said the lady, taking the piece of paper. "Oh dear, how awful for you."

The man frowned thoughtfully. "I don't think the people on the next boat are up yet," he said, glancing over. The boat at the end still had its curtains drawn and there was no noise from it at all. "Want us to tell them for you?"

"Please." Grandad nodded. "Thanks, you've been really helpful."

Anna tried to smile at the friendly

couple, but she just couldn't make her face do it. "Are we going now?" she asked Grandad, as she climbed back on to the *Hummingbird*.

Grandad nodded and headed for the stern to start the engine. "Yes, I think it's best. We can come back and spend the whole day here looking if we need to. But I'm sure we won't," he added quickly.

Anna could tell he didn't believe that at all, but she was just grateful to him for saying it.

"I wouldn't be surprised if we had a call from your mum and dad really soon," Gran said comfortingly. "I'm sure they'll have news."

"The engine's warmed up enough now," Grandad called from the stern, and Anna took one last, hopeful look along the bank, but no feathery, dark-red dog came running out to her.

"Let's go," she said. Then she coughed to clear her throat and said it again, loud enough to be heard over the engine this time. "The sooner we go, the sooner we can come back and start looking for Fred again."

Grandad nodded, and Anna hopped over on to the towpath to cast off the mooring ropes. Then she climbed back on to the bow deck. Gran had gone into the cabin, but Anna decided to stay out on deck. She felt like being on her own for a bit.

"We'll be back really soon, Fred," she whispered. "I'm not leaving you behind. We're coming back to find you."

Chapter Eight

Sunny felt the boat start to move away from the bank. He climbed out of his basket and came to stand next to Anna, putting his paws up on the bench seat that ran round the side of the bow and peering over the side.

Anna stroked his black head and sighed. "I wish you could help us find Fred, Sunny. Couldn't you sniff him out for me?" Then she frowned. "I wonder if you could? I'll have to ask Grandad. If you did, I promise we'd take him straight home – no more Fred trying to make you play chase. Honest."

Then she sniffed. She'd give anything to be chasing around the park with Fred now. She wouldn't even mind being stuck at home, bored, while Mum was working, just as long as Fred was there with her.

"I shouldn't have said yes to coming on the boat, should I?" she said to Sunny, tears rolling slowly down her cheeks. "It wasn't fair on you or Fred." She gave Sunny a last pat, and then climbed up on to the little bench. She lifted her hand to shield her eyes from the sun, scanning the bank eagerly as they drew away into the middle of the canal and began to sail slowly around the bend. The other boats hid the bank, and Anna suddenly couldn't bear that they were leaving. Fred was still there, somewhere! "Fred!" she yelled, again and again. But he didn't come. Anna put her hands over her eyes and cried.

Fred felt the thrumming sound of the engine more than he heard it. He was so tired after his frightened dash away through the woods, and his hours cramped up underneath the tree, that he'd slept far later than he usually would.

His first thought when the engine growled was that he was very, very hungry and why hadn't Anna come to find him for some breakfast? He would go and look for her right now. He twitched and stretched under the canvas awning, pushing his front paws out along the deck. But the feel of the heavy canvas over his head and shoulders was wrong, and his legs still ached a little. As he began to wake up properly, he had the feeling that something wasn't right.

Then he remembered.

He wasn't with Anna. He was on the other boat, hiding. The wrong boat! And that growling loudness was the sound that boats made when they moved! He had to get off, now, before this boat took him away from Anna!

Frantically, he scrambled out from beneath the awning and dashed to the side of the boat. Then a great shudder of relief ran through him, and his tail swished gladly back and forth. The boat was still moored up against the bank. It hadn't moved, even though he'd heard the engine noise.

Fred half-jumped, half-scrabbled his way out on to the bank. He needed to get back to Anna. Even if it meant Sunny growling at him and Grandad and everyone else being angry, he didn't care. Anna was what mattered. Even if she was cross with him, he wouldn't mind, as long as she was there. He'd missed her, and he was hungry, and he wanted *her* to feed him. No one else.

Fred pranced down the towpath, his tail wafting happily. Should he jump straight back on to the boat, or should he bark and let Anna see him and call him on board? If he barked, he might set Sunny off growling at him. Perhaps it would be best to just jump into that little bit of the boat outside the door, and sit quietly and wait?

He hurried eagerly along past another boat and looked curiously at the people sitting on it. The lady got to her feet and waved her arms at him. But Fred ran on.

Then he stopped, staring at the space where Anna's boat was meant to be.

They had gone. Without him.

Anna had left him behind. Fred walked to the edge of the bank, somehow hoping that he was wrong and the boat was there after all. But it definitely wasn't. That had been the engine noise he'd heard – it had been them leaving.

He could still hear it. Not too loud, but there. Perhaps they had only just gone? Fred leaned out over the edge of the bank, trying to see, his paws scrabbling on the grass. There they were! He could even just make out Anna, standing at the front of the boat.

He was about to bark, to tell her to come back for him, when he saw that Sunny was with her. She was stroking his head. Running her fingers over Sunny's ears, the way she did with his.

Fred watched, his tail sinking down between his legs. She wanted Sunny instead of him. He had caused so much trouble, and knocked things over, and made people shout at him. Anna's mum and dad had taken him away because she didn't want him any more.

But then, just as the boat began to turn, Anna suddenly stepped up on to something. Fred could see her better now. Sunny disappeared, and Anna stood there, peering at the bank as though she was looking for something.

For him?

She was crying. She was brushing tears away from her eyes, and she was calling... He could only just hear her over the engine noise, but he was sure that she was. Her voice had gone all growly and strange – the way it was when she was upset.

Fred barked and whipped round, racing down the bank after them. He hardly heard the lady on the next boat calling him frantically as she climbed over on to the bank. He didn't realize that she was trying to catch him as he shot past her. He only knew that he had to get to Anna.

The *Hummingbird* was pulling around the shallow bend in the canal now. Fred barked and barked as he ran, and he saw Anna look round and spot him.

"Fred!" she screamed excitedly. "Grandad, stop! Fred's there!"

Grandad turned to look at the bank and swung the tiller over to move in towards it. But the heavy boat took time to change course, and to Fred it didn't seem to be changing direction at all. He could see that Anna was shouting and waving, and she didn't look cross with him at all. But why wasn't she coming back for him?

Maybe she couldn't…?

Fred watched the boat for a couple more seconds, seeing it still drawing further down the canal. Taking Anna away from him.

Then he jumped into the water.

The water was cold and dark and unwelcoming and he didn't want to be in it at all. But if it was the only way he could get back to Anna, then that was what he would do.

He paddled away with his front paws. This was the first time he had ever been in deep water, and he could feel the weight of it in his coat, dragging him down. And no matter how hard he tried, he didn't seem to be getting very far. The cold seemed to sink straight into his cramped legs, but he kept paddling as hard as he could.

"He's in the water!" Anna screamed. "Grandad, where's the life-ring?" But

Grandad couldn't hear her shouting over the noise of the engine. Anna would have to fetch the life-ring herself. There was no time to lose. She spotted the life-ring attached to the roof and leaned over to reach it.

Grandad had told her never to walk round the narrow shelf that ran round the outside of the boat, but it was the only way she could get close enough to Fred to throw him the heavy life-ring. She hooked it over her arm and stepped out on to the shelf, gripping the rail that ran along the roof of the boat.

As she edged her way round, she could see Fred struggling as he hit the *Hummingbird*'s wake. He gasped and snorted as he swallowed a great mouthful of water.

"I think he's sinking," Anna wailed, clinging on to the rail with one hand. She threw the life-ring as close to Fred as she could, but it fell short. She started to haul it back, glancing worriedly at Fred still struggling in the rough water thrown up behind the boat.

Maybe I should just go in after him, Anna thought, starting to pull off her shoes. She could swim pretty well, even though she knew the canal was nothing like a nice heated swimming pool. Grandad could throw her the life-ring and pull them both in. There was no way she was going to let Fred drown.

But then a black shape shot past her and there was another huge splash, followed by a steady sound of paddling, as Sunny cut through the water.

"Go on, Sunny!" Anna yelled.

Gran hurried out on to the bow deck. "What's going on? I just saw Sunny jump into the canal! Anna, come back down off there!"

"It's Fred!" Anna pointed into the water. "Sunny's rescuing him!"

"Oh my goodness," Gran murmured. "Geoff, look!" she called, banging on the cabin roof. "The dogs are in the canal."

Grandad looked out across the water and his eyes widened. He waved back and steered the boat into the bank.

They all watched as Sunny paddled calmly round behind the boat and up to Fred, who was gasping and struggling in the cold water. The puppy rolled his eyes sideways, wondering what Sunny was doing. He whined as he felt Sunny grab the folds of skin at the scruff of his neck. But he didn't pull away. He could feel that Sunny was helping him. Once he'd got a good hold on Fred, Sunny turned, swimming him back towards the bank.

Anna jumped off the boat as soon as it drew into the side, stumbling as she hit the grass.

"Go and help them," Gran called, grabbing the ropes and stepping after her. "Don't worry. I'll hold on to these."

Grandad shut off the engine and jumped after Anna, and they ran down the bank, just as Sunny and Fred were reaching the side.

"Good dog, Sunny! Come on!" Grandad yelled. "Good boy!"

"Come on, Fred!" Anna called, watching him anxiously. He was so still in Sunny's grip, she couldn't even tell if he was breathing. But as Sunny bumped him gently against the bank, Fred seemed to wake up, scrabbling frantically for dry land. Grandad put his arms under Fred's front legs and hauled him on to the bank, where Fred wriggled gratefully on to Anna's knees. She hugged him tightly.

Sunny leaped out with a helping heave from Grandad and shook himself all over. Then he leaned down and sniffed at Fred, nudging him up.

Fred struggled up obediently, shaking the water out of his coat. Sunny pulled at the leg of Anna's jeans with his teeth, so that she got to her feet, too. Then he set off back to the boat, herding them like a sheepdog, circling round Fred and Anna as they walked back down the towpath.

"What are you doing, Sunny?" Anna giggled.

"He wants everybody safely back on the boat," Grandad said, chuckling.

"He rescued Fred," Anna murmured. She could feel her cold, damp dog shivering against her legs. She was almost sure that Fred wouldn't have made it out of the canal on his own. And she was only realizing now how amazing the rescue had been.

"Sunny doesn't even like Fred!"

Grandad nodded thoughtfully. "He may not like Fred fussing at him, but Fred's part of his family, I suppose."

"I've got towels," Gran called. "I've tied the boat to those trees, just for the minute. Come inside. We'll get the dogs dried off and I'll make some tea."

Sunny stood watchfully by as Anna helped Fred back on to the boat. Then she and Grandad dried the dogs with the old towels Gran had found.

Gran passed Anna a mug of sweet hot chocolate, and looked down worriedly at the two dogs. "I wish we could give them a hot drink, too."

"Fred looks a lot better now he's drier," Anna said, sipping at her hot chocolate. Fred was leaning against her lovingly and she could feel that he wasn't shivering so much. "Oh! We have to call Mum and Dad! We have to tell them we've got Fred back. And that Sunny's a hero dog."

Sunny shook his way out of the towel that Grandad had wrapped round him and stood up, shaking his ears as though they still felt watery. Then he nudged Fred with his muzzle again.

Fred wriggled back to his feet. He licked Anna's cheek lovingly, but he followed Sunny into the saloon, towards Sunny's big wicker basket. Fred stood looking at it uncertainly, his tail waving a little. He knew he wasn't meant to go in Sunny's basket. But the bigger dog pushed him gently into it and climbed in after him, curling up round the Setter puppy as though he was trying to keep him warm.

Sunny glanced at them all, and then let out a deep, huffing sigh and closed his eyes, as though he was finally happy with where everyone was.

"Look at them!" Anna whispered, crouching down to see. "You're right, Grandad. Sunny's decided that Fred's his family now."

Fred peered over the edge of the basket, making sure Anna was still there. He stretched, and wriggled a little, and licked her hand. He was back, and Anna was with him, and everything was all right. Then he snuggled up against the big dog and went to sleep.

The Scruffy Puppy

For everyone at Park Lane Primary School – and especially for Class 3S and 3R!

Chapter One

Bella couldn't help doing a sort of hopping little dance as they went up the steps at the front of the animal shelter. She was just too excited to walk sensibly. She had been waiting so long for this day. It had been weeks and weeks since Mum and Dad had first started talking seriously about getting a dog, and before that Bella had been trying to persuade them for *years*.

Still, they were really here, walking into Redlands Animal Shelter to find a dog who could be their very own.

"What sort of dog do you think we'll get?" she asked suddenly, turning round on the top step, and looking at her mum and dad, and Tom, her older brother. They were all following behind as she had run ahead of them from the car. Bella had wanted to ask this question – and lots of others – ever since Mum had told them about the trip to the animal shelter earlier in the week. But she hadn't quite dared. What if they couldn't decide on a favourite breed and gave up on the whole idea? Even now, she glanced anxiously from Mum to Dad to Tom, wondering what they

would say. She'd been thinking about it
a lot herself – trying to decide what her
absolute favourite, best, loveliest kind
of dog would be.

She hadn't thought about much else for weeks, actually. Her friend Megan had started to roll her eyes every time Bella mentioned dogs at school, or suggested going to the library to look at dog books again. And Mr Peters, their teacher, had told Bella off for daydreaming at least three times. On the other hand, he had given her a star and two house points for her poem about dogs. So it sort of evened out.

But even after all that, Bella still hadn't decided what her top dog actually was. She knew they were getting their dog from the shelter because buying a dog from a breeder would be very expensive, and Mum and Dad really wanted to give a home to a dog who didn't have one, as well. So in a way, it was good that she hadn't set her heart on one particular breed, because the chances of that exact breed being at the shelter were probably small. Still, wasn't it a bit strange that she couldn't decide what her favourite dog really was, when she could choose from any that she liked? She knew what the problem was – it was just that she liked them *all*...

"If there was every sort of dog at the shelter, what would your favourite be?" she asked her mum. "I know it won't be there," she added hurriedly. "I'm just interested."

Mum smiled at her. "I'd been wondering when you'd ask that. I was a bit surprised that you hadn't been on the computer, looking at dog websites and working out exactly what sort of dog you'd like."

Bella gave her a little embarrassed smile. "That's just what I have been doing!" she admitted. "But I can't decide!"

Mum ruffled Bella's hair as she opened the door to the shelter's reception area. "If I could have any dog in the world, I'd like something quite little and cute. Maybe a dachshund."

"Is that a sausage dog?" Tom asked suspiciously. "I don't want a sausage dog. My mates would laugh. Something big would be cool." He grinned. "I really like those big hairy things."

Bella rolled her eyes. "Great description. Which big hairy things?"

"You know. The ones in the paint ads."

"Oh! An Old English Sheepdog!"

Bella nodded excitedly. "They're gorgeous."

"Sorry, you two." Dad shook his head at Bella and Tom. "I shouldn't think there'll be an Old English Sheepdog here, or even a dachshund. I should think most of the dogs will be strays. Mixed breeds, probably."

Bella nodded. Mum was over by the reception desk now, explaining that they'd like to look at dogs for adoption. Bella was so happy, she couldn't keep still. She had to keep talking, or she might burst with excitement. "What sort of dog would you like, Dad?"

"Mmm." Dad frowned. "I fancy something quite big. I like the idea of taking a dog when I go running."

Tom snorted. "So, a greyhound then."

Their dad was really tall and he liked to go on long runs. He had entered the marathon before – they'd all gone up to London to watch him.

Bella shook her head. "I don't know about a greyhound, Dad. I'm not sure they could keep up with you. They're more about going super-fast, but only for a short time. And anyway, if there was a greyhound here, it might be an ex-racing dog." She frowned, and stood still for a minute. "And they're really sad. The owners just dump them when they can't race any more, and they've never had a proper home, or been looked after. They've all got terrible teeth, because the owners never took real care of them. I read about one who had to have all his teeth taken out."

Dad sighed. "I think quite a few of the dogs here might have sad stories, Bella. We just have to think that at least we're going to give one of them a home." He put an arm round her shoulders. "So, what do you think? Great, big, hairy dog? Tiny little fluffy thing?"

Bella sighed.

"I just don't know! I keep trying to imagine myself with different sorts of dog, but I like all of them..." She smiled up at her dad. "When we see them for real, it'll be different, won't it? We'll know which is the perfect dog for us. I'm sure we will."

"How are we ever going to choose?" Bella said helplessly. There were so many dogs, and most of them were really excited to see visitors. They jumped up from their beds, and hurried over to the wire netting in the front of the pens, scrabbling madly, and begging to be stroked, loved, taken home. There were just a few who didn't bother getting up, and Bella thought that they were even sadder. Those dogs must have been at the shelter so long that they knew it was no use. No one was ever going to want them. Their hopeless eyes made her want to cry.

The worst thing was that she could see that her family couldn't take them, either. They were mostly elderly, and didn't look like they'd want to go for runs with Dad, or play around in the garden with her and Tom. But she wished she could be the one to make them happy.

"Are you OK?" One of the centre staff stopped next to her, smiling. She had a badge on that said "Jo – Manager".

Bella gulped. "Yes. I suppose. It's just so sad. Some of the dogs look like they've given up."

Jo sighed. "I know. But it's not completely hopeless, you know. We do find almost all of them homes in the end, even though it can take a long time. Elderly dogs can be great, gentle pets."

She smiled at Bella. "I should think you and your family would like something a bit bouncier, though."

"Yes, please." Bella nodded. "I don't really mind about what breed or anything. I just want to have a dog of our own."

Jo looked at her thoughtfully. "Did you see Sid?"

Bella frowned. "I don't think so. Is he up there somewhere?" She pointed further down the line of pens, where her dad and Tom were crouched down looking in at a big Boxer, who was barking as if he would burst with excitement.

"No, no, you've gone past him. Here." Jo led Bella back a couple of pens, and stopped so she could peer in.

The basket was in the corner of the pen, and all Bella could see was a fuzzy brown and white back.

Jo chuckled. "He could sleep for England, this one. But when he's awake, he's a cutie. Well…" she paused. "He *is* cute. But he's not exactly the best-looking dog in the world. I have to admit, most people pass him over. But I think he's lovely. I'd take him home myself if I didn't have four cats already."

"Has he been here for ages?" Bella asked, crouching down to look at the brown and white furry lump in the basket.

"About, um, four months." Jo sighed. "He's starting to give up, which is so sad. I think he sleeps so much because he really hates being here. He's lovely and affectionate with the staff, but he wants space to run in. A bit of time in the exercise yard just isn't enough."

"My dad really wants a dog who could go running with him," Bella said hopefully. "And my mum just wants a dog who isn't too massive. Sid doesn't look that big. Is he?" She wrapped her fingers round the wire, staring in, and wishing Sid would wake up. The fuzzy white back twitched and wriggled a bit.

"No, he's some sort of terrier cross. Medium-sized, but with longish legs. And even though he's still very young, I don't think he'll get much bigger."

"You mean he's a puppy?" Bella asked excitedly. She hadn't expected they'd be able to get a young dog. Mum and Dad had explained that most of the dogs at the shelter would already have had one owner.

Jo smiled. "Well, let's just say he's a teenager."

"Oh, I wish he'd wake up and come and see me," Bella sighed.

Inside the pen, Sid heard the voices. The nice one, who always stroked him even more than the others when she brought his food. She always scratched his ears, and chatted, and he could tell she liked him. She was talking to someone that he hadn't heard before, though. His ears twitched thoughtfully, and he wondered if it was one of the people who took dogs away. Someone had taken the young Staffie in the opposite pen only yesterday. But even though people looked into his enclosure, they didn't usually want the door opened so they could meet him. He'd stopped bothering to wag his tail and give them hopeful looks. None of them really seemed to see him anyway.

His ears flattened and he wriggled round in his basket a bit. He would go back to sleep, until it was time for food.

"Oh! I thought he was going to wake up!" the young girl said.

The voice sounded sad, and Sid's ears pricked up again. He couldn't help it. He glanced over his shoulder and saw the nice woman there with a girl beside her, crouched by the wire and staring at him.

"He *is* awake!" the girl said excitedly. "Oh, how could anyone not find him cute? He's gorgeous! Look at his beautiful ears!"

The brown and white dog looked like a sort of wiry-haired terrier, but his mad, frizzy ears had come from somewhere else entirely. Maybe a spaniel, or something little and fluffy like a Papillon? The ones with the ears like butterflies? Or maybe a poodle? Bella wasn't sure, but she loved them. They made him look like a dog who'd been put together from bits. As he got up and came cautiously towards them, she saw that he had a mad plumy tail as well. He walked over to the wire, slowly, and his tail began to waft from side to side.

"Hello!" Bella breathed. "Oh, aren't you lovely?" She glanced up at Jo. "Is it OK to put my fingers through the wire? So I can stroke him?" she asked.

"Sure, as long as you're gentle – Sid's very friendly," Jo answered.

Bella slipped her fingers through the netting, and giggled as Sid came closer and licked at them curiously. "That tickles! Hello, sweetheart." Carefully, slowly, she reached her fingers round

to rub under his chin. All the dogs she'd met before loved that. It seemed that Sid did, too. He closed his eyes and sighed blissfully.

"Please can we open the pen? So I can meet him properly?" Bella whispered to Jo.

Jo smiled at her. "Hadn't we better see what your mum and dad think first?" she said.

"Oh! Oh, yes, I forgot. I'll get them! I'm sure they'll love him. I'll be back in a minute, Sid." And Bella jumped up, hurrying away between the pens. The lady on reception had told them not to run, in case it upset the dogs, but she just couldn't help going fast.

Sid sighed and his tail dropped down. His ears sagged as well and he turned to trail back to his basket. It had been stupid to think that the girl had liked him. She had fussed over him and rubbed his chin in just his favourite place, but then she had vanished.

"Hey…" Jo called gently. "She's only gone to find her mum and dad. She's coming back. Sid… Don't be sad, my lovely."

But Sid had gone back to his basket and curled up determinedly. He wasn't listening.

Chapter Two

"Well, he doesn't look very friendly," Mum said rather doubtfully.

"Oh, but he is! Well, he was…" Bella pleaded. "You tell them," she said, turning to Jo.

"He's a lovely dog, but he's been here a while and he's not been adopted," Jo explained. "Some dogs stop bothering to try and say hello to everyone."

"Oh..." Bella saw her mum's face crumple a little. Her mum was just as soppy as she was. A dog who thought he'd never have a proper home was making them both want to cry.

"We could at least open the pen and meet him properly, couldn't we?" Bella asked, fixing her eyes on her mum.

"Oh, yes," Mum nodded.

Sid was still in his basket, but his ears were twitching frantically. There were lots of people outside his pen now – he could hear them. Were they talking about him? He popped his head up a fraction and darted a glance across the pen.

"Aw, look at him!" Bella's mum laughed. "Look at those ears!"

"Exactly!" Bella beamed at her.

"Isn't he a bit ... scruffy-looking?" Dad said, coming up behind them with Tom.

Bella glared at him. "He's gorgeous!"

"He does have a lovely personality," Jo put in as she opened the pen. "Very friendly, and he likes lots of exercise. Bella said you like to run? He'd be over the moon at that. He's got great long legs..."

Dad smiled. "Let's meet him then."

Sid stood up in his basket, his tail waving uncertainly back and forth. They were definitely getting him out! His tail wagged faster and faster, and when Jo called, "Sid! Sid, here boy!" he shot out of the basket so fast he skidded over the tiled floor, and almost crashed into Dad's feet.

"Hello!" Dad laughed. "All right, you're keen, aren't you!" He rubbed Sid's huge feathery ears, while Bella scratched him under the chin again. Sid stood there, practically dribbling with pleasure.

"What do you think, Tom?" Mum asked.

Tom was grinning. "He's great. Dad, you know he's about to drool on your trainers?" Tom crouched down by Sid and stroked his back. "He's a weird mix, isn't he. Short fur and fluffy ears. But he's really friendly."

Bella sighed happily, and Sid looked up at her with shy black eyes. "I told you, didn't I," she whispered, as Dad stood up and began to talk to Jo about dates for bringing Sid home with them. "I said they'd love you, and I was right!"

"He's so sweet," Bella told Megan as they put their coats away. She'd been waiting for her friend by the gate, but Megan hadn't arrived until just before the bell. Bella should have known – it was the same every morning – but she'd been desperate to tell Megan about Sid.

"The lady from the shelter's coming over after school to see the house—"

"What for?" Megan asked, sounding surprised.

"Oh, to make sure it's a proper home for a dog. That we've got a bit of garden, and no young children, things like that."

"I'd have thought they couldn't be that picky." Megan shrugged. "If they're just stray dogs."

"Well, they've got to find them nice homes," Bella pointed out, feeling a

287

bit hurt. "Or they'll only end up back at the shelter again, won't they."

"Mmm, suppose so. Did you do that maths homework?"

"Yes." Bella was about to start telling Megan how beautiful Sid's ears were, but her friend was already hurrying out of the cloakroom. Bella sighed. Maybe she was going on about Sid a bit too much. But how could she stop talking about him when he was so gorgeous?

The home visit went well, even though Bella was really nervous. She'd been certain that Jo would find something awful about their house, and say that they couldn't bring Sid home after all.

But Jo seemed to think they'd be brilliant dog owners, especially as Mum worked from home. Bella had shown her a leaflet about dog-training classes, which she'd picked up at the hall where she went for dancing, and Jo had beamed at her.

"Great! You sound as though you're taking it all really seriously. I think Sid shouldn't be too hard to train. He's very good-natured, and he already knows how to sit and walk to heel."

Jo had also told them a little bit of Sid's story. He'd been found abandoned as a puppy, stuffed into a cardboard box at a rubbish dump. Mum had cried when Jo told them that, and Bella had felt like crying, too. How could anyone be so cruel? It had made all of them – Mum, Dad, Bella and Tom – determined to make sure that Sid had the best home ever after such an awful start.

Jo had arranged that they could come and pick Sid up at the weekend – just a week after they'd first seen him. It wasn't really all that long to wait, but for Bella, it seemed as though the week lasted forever. She dashed out of school on Friday afternoon with just the speediest, "Bye! Have a nice weekend!" to Megan. She and her mum were meeting Tom up the road at his school. Then they were all going to the pet shop to choose a basket, and the other things that Sid would need once they brought him home.

By the time they got to the shelter at nine o'clock on Saturday morning, Bella had already been up for hours, and she was buzzing with excitement. Today was the day! They were really going to be bringing Sid home.

"I've been making a big fuss of him," Jo said, smiling. "He was a bit down when you left last weekend – he'll be so pleased to see you again."

Bella nodded. She'd been worrying that Sid wouldn't understand they were coming back to get him.

"Dad and I will look through the paperwork," Mum suggested to Bella and Tom. "Why don't you two go and see Sid?"

"Ah, is that a new collar and lead for him?" Jo smiled. "Let's go and get him and put them on. Then we can bring him out here to your mum and dad."

Bella gulped excitedly.

Tom fumbled at the fastening on the collar, undoing it so they were ready to give it to Sid. "This is so cool," he muttered, nudging Bella. "Our own dog!"

"I can't believe it's really happening," Bella whispered back, as they followed Jo down to the pens.

But it was. Sid was there, sitting hopefully by his door, as if he'd heard their voices. When he saw them his tail beat slowly back and forth, and he glanced from Bella to Tom and back to Bella again, as though he wasn't quite sure it was really happening either.

"He's so lovely," Bella murmured, choking up a little bit.

"Don't start crying!" Tom rolled his eyes. "You're as bad as Mum! This is a good thing, Bella! Hey, Sid," he added in a gentle voice. "Look what we brought for you." He held out the lead, and Sid's slowly wagging tail suddenly went about ten times faster.

Jo laughed. "He loves his walks. Or his runs, I should say." She opened the pen door and let Tom slip inside to fuss over Sid, and then put the collar on.

"It looks so nice," Bella said proudly. The collar was a smart blue one that she'd chosen, with a matching lead. Mum had even had their phone number put on the little bone-shaped tag already.

Tom grinned at her, and passed over the lead. "You can take him, Bella. You chose him, after all."

Bella's fingers were shaking as she took the lead, and Sid stared up at her hopefully. His tail was still wagging at top speed. "Are you coming with us, Sid?" she murmured. "Shall we go home?"

Sid sat in his comfy, padded basket, watching solemnly as Bella showed him all the toys they'd bought.

"And look, this is a squeaky bone!" She squeaked it for him and laid it down to join the line with all the others.

"Bella went a bit mad in the pet shop," her mum said, leaning down to stroke his ears. "This is enough for about three dogs, isn't it, Sid!"

Sid recognized his name, and wagged his tail a bit, even though he didn't know what they were talking about.

"I hope he's OK," Bella murmured worriedly. "He's so quiet."

"A new home is a lot to get used to, I should think," Mum pointed out. "Give him some time."

Sid looked at Bella, her straight blonde hair falling over her face as she crouched down to arrange the toys for him again. He liked her. He liked her a lot. As she came close, he leaned out of the basket and gave her cheek a sweeping, wet lick.

Bella collapsed backwards, giggling, and Sid followed her, planting his hairy white paws on her tummy so he could lick her again.

"Uuuugggh, Sid!" But Bella put her arms round his neck and hugged him. "You silly dog," she told him lovingly, and Sid licked her one more time.

Chapter Three

"Hi! Megan, is that you?" Bella said excitedly into the phone. "We've got him! Sid's at home with us – we brought him home yesterday! Do you want to come round and meet him? Mum says you can." Bella waited expectantly for a voice at the other end, sure that Megan would jump at the chance.

"Actually, sorry, Bella, I can't."

"Oh…" Bella didn't know what to say – she was really disappointed. Megan sounded excited about something, though. There was a bubbly sort of sound to her voice, as if she had a secret.

"Have you got some news?" Bella asked curiously.

"Yes – we've got a dog, too! We got her yesterday. She's a spaniel and we're calling her Coco." Megan's words spilled over each other, she was so eager to tell Bella her news.

For just a moment, Bella felt cross – getting a dog was her special thing. She had been desperate for one for ages. And now Megan had a dog, too, just like that. She knew that Megan's mum and dad gave her loads of things

– whatever she wanted really, because she was an only child and they worried that she was lonely. But why a dog? Bella hadn't even thought Megan liked dogs all that much.

"I didn't know you wanted a dog," she said quietly, trying not to let the things she was thinking show in her voice.

"You kept talking about how brilliant it would be. So – I thought maybe you were right. I begged Dad, and he took me to choose a puppy yesterday."

"What, straight away? You didn't have to have a home visit or anything?"

"Course not!" Megan laughed. "Coco came from a breeder, not a shelter. She's a proper pedigree dog. She was *very* expensive," she added proudly.

"Oh…" Bella frowned. Sid hadn't been expensive. They'd paid a donation to the shelter, to help look after the other dogs, but that was all… Bella chewed her lip worriedly, and then gasped in surprise as a warm weight settled on her feet.

Sid stared up at her lovingly, and Bella giggled and tickled his tummy with her bare toes. She was being stupid. It was great that Megan had a dog, too. "Maybe we can all go to the park this afternoon!" she suggested excitedly. "Sid and Coco could make friends."

"I'll ask Mum," Megan said. "Hold on."

Bella waited patiently as she heard her off in the background, talking to her mum. A few moments later, Megan came back to the phone.

"Bella? I forgot, we can't yet," she said. "The breeder said we ought to give her time to adjust to being at home with us. I think it's silly, but Mum says we've got to."

"Oh! OK. Well, I'm sure she's right."

"Suppose so. Anyway, bring a photo of Sid to school, OK? I'll bring one of Coco."

"All right." Bella put the phone back in its cradle on the kitchen windowsill, and reached down to run her hand over Sid's soft ears. "I don't care that you weren't expensive," she whispered. "I think you're perfect."

"Finally!" Tom put his head round the door. "I thought you were never getting off the phone. Mum says we can all go for a—" He eyed Sid carefully and said the last word in a whisper. "Walk."

Even though Tom had whispered the words, Sid still jumped round in a complete circle, ears flapping, his helicopter tail practically lifting him off the ground.

"Well, that's popular." Bella giggled. "Come on then!"

Bella's house was near a small park with a little children's playground and a stretch of grass. There was a bigger one a bit further away, but they decided not to go too far for the first walk.

Bella, Tom and Sid were so excited that it was hard to remember about walking to heel. All three of them just wanted to run. It seemed mean to make Sid walk nicely when it was the first time he'd had a proper walk in ages. The shelter had told them that they used volunteers to take the dogs for walks, but there were never enough to take all the dogs out.

Sid could smell the park – the scent of grass and other dogs, and space to run in. But he did his best to walk next to Bella, the way he'd been taught.

"He's being so good," Dad said, sounding a bit surprised. "I was expecting him to be pulling your arm off, Bella."

Bella nodded. "You're such a good boy. Good *boy*, Sid."

Sid shook his frizzy ears happily and nosed at Bella's leg. The park was really close now. He stopped short as they came up to the gate, gazing at the biggest open space he'd ever seen.

"I think he's too excited to move," Mum said, laughing. "Go on in, Bella. See if he wants to go for a runaround."

Bella nodded and handed the lead to Tom – she didn't want to, but he'd let her take Sid all the way there, so it was his turn. She trotted off backwards, calling gently to Sid. "Here, Sid! Come on! Let's run!"

And a white streak of excited dog raced out across the grass towards Bella, with Tom galloping at the end of his lead.

When Bella arrived at school on Monday morning, for once Megan had actually got there on time.

305

She was sitting on one of the playground benches near the door to their classroom, with an admiring crowd gathered round her.

Bella hurried over, eager to talk about the dogs, and how much fun it was to be an owner at last. But it wasn't easy to get a word in. Megan had a great long string of photos, in a special holder covered in paw prints. She was happily showing them off to all the girls in their class. Bella peered over. Coco did look very, very sweet. She was a little golden Cocker Spaniel, with huge dark-brown eyes and very curly ears. She was wearing a collar made of pink sparkly stones that looked a bit big for her in the photo that Bella could see.

"I've got three little coats for her and four different collars," Megan was saying airily. "She's so pretty, she looks perfect in everything. Oh, hi, Bella! Look, this is Coco!"

"She's so cute." Bella nodded. She could see more of the photos now – one for every different collar and outfit, and quite a few with Coco lined up next to the soft toys on Megan's bed.

That's what Coco's like, Bella thought suddenly. *One of Megan's soft toys*. Bella couldn't say that, though. Not without upsetting Megan. And besides, she felt mean. But she did feel sorry for Coco – she must have been changed in and out of coats and collars all weekend. A puppy wasn't a doll for dressing up.

"She's got a pedigree as well," Megan said proudly. "Lots of her relatives have won prizes – one of them's a Supreme Grand Champion. Coco's really called Golden Daydream of Melton."

Bella giggled. She couldn't help it – it was such a silly-sounding name. But Megan glared at her crossly. "Did you bring a photo of your dog?" she demanded.

"Yes," Bella murmured, suddenly

wondering if she wanted to show Megan right now, with all these girls around. Especially when they'd just been looking at super-pretty Coco. They might not think Sid was very special. In fact, they might think he was downright scruffy.

"Go on, Bella. We want to see! Is your puppy a spaniel, too?" Lara asked. She and Chloe hung around with Megan and Bella a lot, but sometimes Bella wished they didn't. Lara could be mean, and Chloe just giggled and went along with everything that Lara said.

"Yeah, show us!" Chloe said now, giggling.

Bella looked down at her school rucksack, which was a bit chewed round the edges. She'd left it on one of the chairs in the kitchen and Sid had obviously fancied a midnight snack. Mum had said that they'd better not leave anything out in the kitchen overnight from now on. The photo was in the front pocket, but she didn't really want to get it out. What if they laughed at Sid?

"Come on!" Lara huffed. "I bet she hasn't even got a dog at all. She's just making it up to copy Megan."

"I am not!" Bella said furiously. If anything it was the other way round. She glared at Lara and Megan. "I told you about Sid last week, and how we were going to adopt him from the animal shelter. He's a mix of lots of breeds."

"Oh, so he doesn't have a kennel name like Coco, then?" Megan asked.

Bella eyed her. Megan knew quite well that Sid didn't have a fancy kennel name. She was just trying to show Bella up, to look good in front of Lara and Chloe and the  others. Bella pulled the photo of Sid from her rucksack, and held it out.

Lara snorted. "What is *that*?"

"That's Sid," Bella said through her teeth. "He's probably a sort of terrier cross."

"Crossed with a mop?" Lara said, nudging Megan and sniggering. "Bella, that's the oddest dog I've ever seen!"

Bella felt hot tears pricking the back

of her eyes and blinked them away. Chloe and some of the others laughed, but for a second, Bella thought she saw Megan look uncomfortable.

"Isn't it odd?" Lara said, nudging Megan again, and this time Megan nodded and sniggered.

"Well, I think he looks really sweet," someone said behind Bella. She whirled round gratefully, wondering who it was. Not many people would stand up to Lara when she was picking on someone.

It was the new girl, Sarah, and she was peering over Bella's shoulder at the photo of Sid. "His ears are fab," she added. "Maybe there's some poodle in him."

"Yes," Bella agreed gratefully. She

hardly knew Sarah – she'd only started at their school this term. In fact, she wasn't sure she'd ever spoken to her before. But now she wanted to hug her. "I thought so, too. And he's a really fast runner. So maybe some whippet as well."

"You're really lucky having a dog." Sarah sighed. "We live in a flat, so we can't have one."

"Did anyone ask you for your opinion?" Lara snapped. "And who cares if you live in a flat? We certainly don't!"

Bella looked apologetically at Sarah. Sometimes, Lara was totally horrible. But it was just easier to be friends with her than not...

Sarah went pink and started to walk away.

Bella watched her for a second, hesitating, and then grabbed Sarah's arm. "Hey, do you want to come over and meet Sid? On Friday maybe?" she asked. She  could feel Lara and Megan's eyes boring into her back – it was as if their eyes were burning holes in her cardigan. But she didn't care. They were both being mean, and Sarah sounded like she knew about dogs and would be fun to talk to.

Sarah just gazed at her in amazement, and then she nodded.

"Yes, please. I'll have to ask my mum, but I'd love to come and meet him."

A few of the girls who were gathered round the bench whispered and muttered, and Bella caught a couple of doubtful glances aimed at Lara. It was as though the others thought she was being too nasty as well.

"My dad says we can enter Coco in a dog show!" Megan said suddenly behind them, trying to get everyone's attention back. "And she'll probably win, because she's really well-bred."

"Not like that thing Bella's calling a dog," Lara sniggered.

Bella dug her fingernails into her palms. She was sick of Lara being horrid, and Megan sucking up to her. "Actually, Sid's going to be in a show,

315

too!" she snapped at Megan.

Then Bella stomped away, wishing she hadn't said anything. She could hear them all sniggering, and there was no way Sid was going to be in a dog show – after all, where would she ever find one to enter him in?

Chapter Four

Sid prowled backwards and forwards in front of the door, stopping occasionally to sniff the faint breeze that came wafting in round the sides. Then he flopped down on the doormat with a huge sigh.

When would they be back? Bella and Tom had been away all day, and even though their mum had been around, she had been sitting quietly and not wanting to play. She would pet him if he whined at her, but then she went back to the pieces of paper she was working on. She had got up to let him out into the garden a couple of times, and she had taken him for a quick walk at lunch, but she hadn't really played. And then she had gone out. He was bored.

Then his ears pricked up. He could hear footsteps! He jumped to his feet and snuffled hopefully at the bottom of the door. Yes! It was Bella – he could hear her voice. Sid let out a delighted yap, and then he heard Bella, excited and running.

"Listen, Tom! He heard us coming. Hi, Sid!"

Sid barked madly, racing round the

hallway so fast he nearly knocked over the basket of scarves and hats by the front door. When the door opened – carefully, because Bella's mum suspected he was probably right behind it – he whirled and bounced around their feet, jumping up and squeaking with joy.

"I don't think he missed us," Tom said in a pretend-sad voice, making Bella laugh.

"It's so nice to see you," Bella murmured, crouching down and hugging Sid. "I can't believe I let Megan and the others make me think you weren't perfect."

It didn't take long for Sid to get used to the pattern of living with a family. Even though there were boring parts when Bella and Tom were away for the whole day at school, he could usually doze through those, or chew his toys. The walks made up for the slow times.

After the first couple of days, Bella

and Tom were allowed to take him out on their own after school. Mum and Dad said it was all right, as long as they stayed together and Tom took his phone – he had got one when he'd gone to secondary school. When they got back, Sid would have a snooze while Bella did her homework, and then they'd go out into the garden and practise training.

Bella was determined that Sid was going to be the most beautifully trained dog ever. She had even bought a book on it with her pocket money, and in a couple of weeks they were going to start classes. Somehow, because he was a bit scruffy-looking, Bella felt that people who met Sid might think he was badly behaved. So she was determined to do her absolute best to make sure that he *wasn't*.

Luckily, Sid really seemed to like the training. Especially the delicious dog treats that Bella used as rewards. She was trying to teach him to sit and stay until she called him, and he was getting quite good at it. Or at least he was while Bella was looking at him. If she turned her back, he would start to creep very, very slowly towards her and then as soon as she turned round again, he would look all innocent.

Bella was keen to teach Sid to come when he was called, so that she could safely let him off the lead in the park. But she had decided to wait until the training classes for that one. She didn't quite trust herself to teach Sid on her own. What if he disappeared off to the other end of the park and wouldn't come back? Or – even worse – he ran out through the gates on to the road?

As much as she loved the training sessions, it was their morning walks that were Bella's favourite. She and Dad had to get up extra early to take Sid out before breakfast, but she didn't mind. It was lovely – there weren't many people around, and they could use Sid's special extending lead, so he could run all across the park. Dad had warned Bella that the walks might not be so much fun in winter when it was cold and dark, but she couldn't imagine not wanting to take Sid out. He loved walks so much and that made her happy.

"Still not bored with getting up early?" Dad asked Bella on Thursday, as she let out a massive yawn on the way to the park.

"No!" Bella shook her head firmly. "I'm just sleepy. I love the walks."

"How's Megan getting on with her new dog?" Dad asked.

Bella nibbled her bottom lip. She didn't want to tell Dad that she'd hardly spoken to Megan since Monday. They had been best friends since they'd started school, and even though Megan annoyed her sometimes, Bella missed her. And she didn't really feel like talking about it. "She's fine."

"Ooooh, watch out, Bella. Another dog coming," her dad said suddenly. "Want me to take the lead?"

Bella shook her head. "No, I'm sure he'll be good. Heel, Sid." She pressed the button on the extending lead that made it go short again and patted her leg, calling encouragingly to Sid. He pattered over to her at once, tail wagging. He'd seen the other dog and he wanted to sniff at him, but Bella was calling.

"Oh, good boy!" Bella rubbed his ears and drew him over to the side of the path so that the lady with the dog – a huge Weimaraner – could get past. But instead, the lady stopped and smiled.

"Have you just got your dog? I haven't seen you out walking him before."

"Yes, we adopted him from Redlands, the shelter," Dad explained.

"He's very sweet! And so well behaved. It's lovely to see you training him to walk properly with you," she added to Bella. "You're obviously working really hard with him. Have a nice morning!"

And she walked on, leaving Dad and Bella staring at each other proudly. Then they both started telling Sid how fabulous he was. "You little star, Sid! Did you hear what she said?"

Sid stared up at them, wondering what all the fuss was about. All he'd done was stand still…

Chapter Five

Bella had chatted to Sarah a few more times since the new girl had stuck up for her on Monday with Megan and the others. But to be honest, she wasn't really looking forward to bringing her home for tea. Mum had been fine with it – she'd said it was good to have lots of different friends, and that it must have been hard for Sarah to start a new school in the middle of the year.

Bella knew that was all true, but it didn't make Sarah any easier to talk to. She was quite shy, Bella decided. She seemed to spend most of her break and lunchtimes reading on one of the benches in the playground. Bella had stopped to talk to her whenever she'd gone past, but Sarah just wasn't all that chatty.

So the walk home from school was a bit awkward. Mum did her best, asking Sarah about why they'd moved (because her mum had got a new job) and whether she liked her new flat (yes, but she wished they had a garden). But it was hard to keep the conversation going, and Bella couldn't help wishing that she was back being friends with Megan again, and that it was Megan who was coming home to tea instead.

As they walked into the front garden, the sound of barking greeted them. "I can hear Sid," Mum said, laughing. "He can always tell we're coming, Sarah. He gets all excited – it's lovely. Although I have to say, he's far more excited when it's Bella or Tom coming than he is for me!"

Sarah nodded and she suddenly looked a lot less shy. "I can hear him, too," she said, laughing. "That squeaky noise! And a sort of scrabbling?"

Bella giggled. "He's trying to dig under the front door," she explained. "He always does it, even though you'd think by now he'd have worked out he never gets anywhere. Hey, Sid!"

Mum slid the key in the lock, and before they knew it Sid was waltzing delightedly about on the front doorstep, dashing from Bella to Mum and back again. He sniffed at Bella and licked her fingers lovingly. Then he shot over to Mum to make sure she knew he loved her, too. He was so excited that it took him a few seconds to notice Sarah. But then he spotted her and went into his funny meeting-new-people pose.

"Oh, look, he did this when Gran came over!" Bella smiled at Sarah. "He goes all shy – watch him."

Sid put his head on one side and looked up quietly at Sarah, peering at her through his big white eyebrows and scraping one paw on the tiled doorstep.

"It's like he wants to ask you to dance, but he's not quite brave enough," Mum said, laughing. "Do you like dogs, Sarah?"

"I love them!" Sarah's eyes were sparkling, and she looked hopefully at Bella. "Is it OK if I stroke him? Will he mind?"

"Oh no, he's really friendly," Bella said proudly. "Look, Sid, this is Sarah. He loves being tickled under the chin," she added.

Sarah crouched down and petted Sid, scratching him under the chin so his eyes closed blissfully, rubbing his ears, and then running her hand all down his spine so that he wriggled in delight.

"Wow, he loves that!" Bella said. She frowned at Sarah. "You're so good with him – but I thought you didn't have a dog?"

"I don't." Sarah looked up at her sadly. "But back at my old house we lived really close to my grandad, and he's got a gorgeous dog. Alfie. He's a collie cross. I used to go on walks with him and Grandad all the time."

"You must miss him," Bella said, thinking how much she would miss Sid, and she'd only had him a week. "Oh, and your grandad, too, of course."

"Yeah." Sarah nodded sadly. "Grandad emails me photos, but it's not the same."

"Come on in, girls, you're still standing on the doorstep! What about something to drink?"

Somehow that made Bella and Sarah shy with each other again – Mum fussing around, asking Sarah if she'd like apple juice or squash, and maybe a biscuit? It showed up how much they didn't know each other. Once they both had drinks, Bella took Sarah and Sid upstairs to her room.

Otherwise she had a feeling they'd sit at either end of the sofa and not know what to say.

Sarah sat on the beanbag with Sid in front of her, eyeing her biscuit.

"Don't get it anywhere near his nose," Bella warned her. "I'm training him, but he's not an angel. He loves biscuits." She picked up a little tin from her desk. "Do you want to give him one of these? They're chews – they're supposed to be good for his teeth." She handed one of the little bone-shaped chews to Sarah and watched her feeding it to Sid.

Sid gobbled it down, and then flopped on to the floor, resting his nose on Sarah's feet, just in case she felt like giving him another treat.

"He really likes you," whispered Bella.

"I like him, too." Sarah glanced up at her shyly. "Thanks for letting me come over. I-I was a bit surprised when you asked me. I mean, because you're friends with Megan and Lara and Chloe."

Bella shrugged. "Not at the moment I'm not. Megan's hardly spoken to me all week, and Lara was so horrible about Sid, I don't think I ever want to talk to her again."

Sarah shuddered. "I don't really like her. She ... she just knows the absolute meanest thing to say. The best way to make people miserable."

Bella stared at her. "What did she say to you?" She'd never noticed Lara picking on Sarah.

Sarah shrugged, hunching up her shoulders. "Stuff about how I'd never have any friends here," she muttered. "And Megan asked why didn't I go back to my old school."

"Megan did?" Bella murmured, feeling shocked.

"Mmm. That's why I was so surprised when you asked me round. I thought you were like them." Sarah looked at her sideways and added, "Sorry."

"I don't like Lara and Chloe much, either. Megan isn't usually like that, though…" Bella nibbled her thumbnail.

"Well, she is sometimes," she admitted. "But she's fun as well. And most of the time she's nice." She sighed. "Anyway, why did you stick up for me, if you thought I was like Lara?" she asked suddenly.

Sarah grinned at her. "I wasn't sticking up for you. I was sticking up for Sid. And I thought that anybody who was so excited about getting a dog had to have some good points."

"Thanks!" Bella rolled her eyes, and Sarah let out a snort of laughter. This made Bella laugh, too, and then they couldn't stop.

Sid looked up at them both, blinking sleepily, and wondering why they were making so much noise. He sighed and snuggled back on to Sarah's feet.

"Are you really entering Sid into a dog show?" Sarah asked a few minutes later, when they'd just about stopped giggling.

Bella made a face. "I don't know. I only said it because I was so angry with Megan. She was being such a show-off, saying Coco was better than Sid. I didn't even think about what I was saying." She sighed. "She's never going to let me forget about it, you know. She was talking at lunchtime today about the dog show Coco's going to.

338

About how her dad's entered Coco in the puppy class. And then she looked at me and smiled…"

"But you *could* enter Sid into a dog show, too, you know." Sarah said, looking at her excitedly. "Grandad took Alfie to one once, and it had fun classes, like catch the sausage. Alfie won that. He got a rosette and everything."

"Really?" Bella looked at her hopefully. "Maybe there's a show like that we could take Sid to. I bet he'd be *excellent* at catching sausages."

Sid's ears twitched, then he looked up eagerly and bounced to his feet. Sausage was a word he knew.

"See?" Bella started to laugh again, and Sid lay back down with a sigh. He didn't think they had any sausages at all.

Chapter Six

The girls went downstairs to borrow Bella's mum's computer to find out if there was a dog show nearby that they could go to.

"Oh, look, click on that one! That's in Lace Hill, not far away," Sarah pointed out excitedly.

"Yes!" Bella opened up the page, and the two girls peered at it eagerly.

**Lace Hill Dog Club
Annual Show**

Open Show
Novelty Classes
Agility Display
Stalls
Refreshments
Fun Day Out for all the family!

Saturday 22nd March

"That's in a couple of weeks," Bella said thoughtfully. "I bet it's the same one Megan's entering Coco in. She said it was two weeks on Saturday."

"What does 'Open Show' mean?" Sarah asked, frowning.

"It means that any dog can enter – they don't have to have won a show somewhere else already," a voice came from behind them.

Bella and Sarah jumped – they hadn't heard Bella's dad come in, even though Sid was happily sniffing at him. They'd been too busy looking at the website.

"Oh... How did you know that, Dad?" asked Bella.

"I've been to that show before – ages ago, Bella, before you were born. Mum and I went with your gran. They're right, it's a great day out! Some people take it quite seriously, though."

"But there are fun classes, too," Bella said. "It says so. Sarah was telling me about a show she'd been to where the dogs had to catch sausages. It sounded great!"

Her dad laughed and pointed to the computer. "Click on the novelty classes. It should tell you what they are."

Bella clicked where her dad had pointed. The screen flashed up with another page.

"'Waggiest tail' – oh, Sid could win that!" Bella giggled as she read down the list of classes. She turned to look at Sid, who was leaning against Dad's legs and gazing up at him adoringly. Dad had taken to giving him a treat when he came in from work, and Sid wasn't going to let him forget. His fluffy, feathery tail was sweeping back and forth across the carpet.

Sarah laughed. "He has got a lovely big tail. You couldn't miss it! What else is there?"

"'Golden Oldie' – oh, that's for older dogs, of course. 'Prettiest Female', 'Most Handsome Dog'…" Bella looked thoughtfully at Sid. "Well. Maybe not. But he could definitely enter this one – listen! 'Dog that the judges would most like to take home'!"

"It says no dogs under six months can compete at the show," Sarah said. "But Sid's older than that, isn't he?"

"I think so." Bella looked round at Dad questioningly. "They weren't exactly sure at the shelter."

"He's definitely more than six months, Bella, don't worry," said Dad. "Is this the show that you said Megan was entering?" he asked. "Isn't her dog very little? I guess she might just have turned six months old by the time of the show – it's not for another couple of weeks, after all."

Bella nodded. "So, Dad... Would you take me and Sid to the show? Pleeeaase?"

Dad grinned. "I think we should all go. Maybe you could come with us, Sarah. If your mum would let you."

Sarah looked delighted. "I'll ask her. So, which classes do you think you'll enter, Bella?"

Bella frowned at the computer. "I like the idea of 'Best Trick'. Except

345

Sid hasn't got one... But we've got two weeks to learn. I could teach him a trick. I bet I could!"

"Oh, I watched that class at the dog show I went to with Grandad and Alfie!" said Sarah.

"What sort of tricks did the dogs do?" Bella asked anxiously. She wasn't sure she could teach Sid anything really complicated.

"A couple of dogs did a trick where their owners put a treat down right in front of them. Then they had to wait to eat it until their owners gave a signal."

Bella looked at Sid doubtfully. That sounded quite hard. Sid loved his treats. She couldn't imagine him leaving one uneaten.

"The dog that won stood on her hind

legs and walked across the field," Sarah said, frowning as she tried to remember. "Oh, and then at the end, her owner kind of leaned back and stretched his leg out, and she ran up his leg so he could cuddle her! But she was tiny – she was a King Charles spaniel. I think it would be hard for Sid to do that bit. I bet he could walk on his hind legs, though. You'd just need to hold a treat up for him."

Bella looked hopefully at Sarah. "Do you want to come into the garden and see if we can get him to stand up?"

Dad laughed. "If this involves dog treats, it's going to be his new favourite game!"

Because it had been Sarah's idea to teach Sid how to walk on his hind legs, it seemed only fair to let her share in his training. Besides, even though Bella hadn't been looking forward to Sarah coming to her house, they'd ended up having a really good time. Sarah might be quiet, and not at all like Megan, but she was funny, and Bella liked her a lot.

Over the next two weeks they met up a couple of times to go to the park and practise Sid's special trick. Sarah's mum came with them. She said that Sid was the funniest thing she had ever seen. She thought he was bound to win. Sarah came to tea the next Friday as well, and they had another practice session in the garden.

Bella was working at home with Sid,

too, although she had made her mum and dad and Tom promise not to watch them in the garden – she wanted Sid's trick to be a surprise. So of course when she got to school, she couldn't wait to update Sarah on how they were doing – which meant that they spent a lot of time chatting to each other in the corner of the playground, and laughing at whatever silly thing had happened the night before.

That morning, they were giggling together all over again. As they hurried into the cloakroom to hang their coats up, Bella heard an upset sort of yelp behind her, and she swung round in surprise. Sarah was in the doorway, holding her arm, and Megan was next to her. Her old friend looked guilty.

"What did you do, Megan?" Bella demanded. "Sarah, are you OK?"

"Yeah, I just banged my arm…"

"You mean *she* banged it!" Bella snapped. "Did Megan shove you into the door, Sarah? You did, didn't you?" she said, turning angrily to Megan. "What was that for?"

"It was an accident." Megan shrugged, but she didn't look very convincing.

"Yeah, right! Come on, Sarah. We'll ask Mr Peters for an ice pack. Don't let Megan get to you." Bella looked at Megan, skulking miserably by the door, and suddenly realized what was going on. "You're jealous," she gasped, with surprise in her voice. It was true, she was sure.

"What, of you?" Megan was trying to sound sneery, but she only managed to sound as though she was about to cry.

"You're jealous because I'm friends with someone else," said Bella. "Why don't you go and hang around with Lara and Chloe." She shook her head crossly, but as she walked with Sarah down the corridor to their classroom, she glanced back. Megan was actually crying.

Bella felt bad. She had been friends with Megan for years. Even though Megan was being totally horrible, she still couldn't help worrying about her.

Chapter Seven

Bella knew that she ought to talk to Megan, but Megan had said such mean things about Sid and about Sarah, too. She had started it all so Bella thought it should be up to her to make friends again. She didn't sit on the same table as Megan in class, so it wasn't as if they had to talk to each other. Bella just had to keep out of her way.

And as it turned out, she managed to get as far as the day of the dog show without saying anything to Megan at all. It definitely was the Lace Hill Show that Megan and Coco were going to – Bella had heard her telling Lara more about it.

Bella and Dad had decided that they would just go for three classes – 'Waggiest Tail', 'Dog the Judges Would Most Like to Take Home', and 'Best Trick'.

Sarah was coming with them to the show, so her mum dropped her off after breakfast. She had a bag with her, and she looked excited. "How's Sid? Is he nervous?" she asked.

Bella shook her head. "No, he's fast asleep in the kitchen. He hasn't got a clue what's going on. I am, though. I'm sure he's going to do something awful, like wee up the judge's leg, or something. What's in the bag?"

"Just my purse – Mum said there might be fun stalls to look at. I can't wait!"

Mum came into the hallway. "Hello, Sarah! We'd better hurry, girls. You want to get there and see what's going on before the classes start, don't you? And we've got to get Sid into his travel crate – you know how long that takes."

Bella made a face.

"Doesn't he like it?" Sarah asked.

"He goes all mad and wriggly as soon as he sees it, but I think it's more that he's excited about going to places. So far he's only been to the woods in the car, and he loves it there, so it makes him a bit hyper."

They walked out of the front door, and Dad opened the car boot. Sid's ears seemed to go frizzier than ever, and he let out a string of excited yelps before whirling round and round on the end of his lead, nearly tripping Bella up.

"See?" Bella

sighed. "I hope he doesn't get this excited at the show."

"I've got a secret weapon to get him in there." Dad sprinkled a few dog treats on the floor of the travel cage. "Hey, Sid, look!"

Sid sniffed, and jumped straight into the travel cage. He sat, gazing out of the window and panting happily as they set off. He loved the car – and his crate now smelled deliciously of chicken-flavour crunchies.

"Gosh, it's really big…" Bella murmured nervously. "So many people."

"And dogs. Oh, look at that gorgeous sausage dog! In that lady's bag, look!"

357

Sarah pointed at the lady walking past, whose bag had a head sticking out one end, and a tail at the other. "We need to find the registration tent and put Sid's name down."

Mum set off towards a white tent, and the others hurried after her. Bella and Sarah couldn't keep up – Sid wanted to stop and sniff everything.

"Bella, look! There's Megan," Sarah whispered, and Bella looked round.

"Oh, wow. And that's Coco. She really is cute."

Megan was standing by one of the fenced-off rings with her dad, and Coco on her pink lead. Coco looked beautiful, with her shiny golden coat and sparkly collar, but she was dancing about, and a couple of times she almost tripped people up. Megan had to keep pulling her back and apologizing, and her dad looked annoyed.

"Coco, sit!" Megan hissed, but Coco wasn't listening at all.

Bella looked down at Sid proudly. He was naughty sometimes – especially about getting in the car – but now he was walking beautifully by her side.

Bella's dad waved to Megan, and she stared back at him, looking embarrassed. But the two dads didn't know that Bella and Megan weren't talking, and they started chatting, while Coco sniffed at Sid in a friendly sort of way.

Sid looked up at Bella, not quite sure what he was supposed to do. He hadn't met many other dogs since he'd left the shelter.

Bella patted him. "Good boy. Coco's just saying hello."

But Megan scowled and hauled Coco away from Sid, walking further down the fenced ring, with Coco pulling back on her lead all the way.

Bella looked at Sarah and shrugged her shoulders.

Bella's dad raised his eyebrows at Bella and told Megan's dad they'd better go and register for the classes.

"Why was Megan so off with you? What was all that about?" he asked Bella, as soon as they were out of earshot.

Bella shrugged, embarrassed, and Sarah explained for her.

"Megan and Lara were making jokes about Sid being odd, and not a proper pedigree dog like Coco. But did you see Coco getting into trouble? Sid's way better behaved, Bella. You should be proud of him."

"I noticed Coco messing about, too," Dad agreed. "Anyway, I'm sure you and Megan can sort it out, Bella – you've known each other such a long time."

"I know." Bella sighed. "But it wasn't just Sid she was mean about, Dad. She's been cruel to Sarah, too. Oh, I'll talk to her. But not today."

"Are you all right?" Sarah whispered, as Bella stood at the edge of the ring.

"Just a bit nervous," Bella gulped. "I'm glad it's 'Best Trick' first. I'm not so worried about the others. I hope Sid isn't scared by all the noise, though – we should have got Tom to play the guitar or something while we were practising."

"He'll be fab, you both will. Oh, I think it's your turn."

Bella heard her name called, and she grinned nervously at Mum, Dad, Tom and Sarah, who had really good places at the front to watch.

"And this is Bella Pascoe, with her cross-breed, Sid! And he really is a character – look at him!" The announcer sounded as though he was trying not to laugh, and Bella looked down at Sid in surprise. He didn't seem to be at all worried about the audience.

Sid could hear people clapping and laughing and he glanced around the ring. This was nice! Lots of people were looking at him. He stepped out smartly, his tail swishing and his ears pricked at a jaunty angle.

Bella stopped in the middle of the ring and Sid looked up at her with hopeful eyes. He could smell that she had treats. He hoped they were going to do the walking on his hind paws – that meant lots of treats. It was his favourite game.

"Come on, Sid, up!" Bella said, holding a treat over his nose, and Sid stood up at once. The treat was just a little higher than his nose, but he knew Bella would give it to him in a minute. He skittered across the ring, and looked round in surprise as everybody started clapping.

"Good boy! And again." Bella led him back across the ring, and this time they stopped in the middle to do a twirl, which made the audience laugh. The laughter was very loud, but it was a good noise and Sid panted happily. Just the last bit now, and then he was pretty sure Bella would give him the whole handful of treats. He watched carefully, waiting for Bella to pat her knees.

365

If he did it too soon, Bella might fall over – that had happened once in the garden.

"Come on, Sid!" Bella patted her knees, and Sid launched himself at her joyfully, leaping into her arms for the big finish.

"Well done!" Bella whispered in his ear, as she fed him all the chicken flavour crunchies, and listened to everybody clapping. "You were great. But you'd better not get any fatter, Sid, or we won't be able to do that last bit…"

"He looks so smart with a red rosette on his collar," Sarah said admiringly. "He ought to have another one for the 'Dog the Judges Would Most Like to Take

Home', though. You were robbed!"

Bella shrugged. "I knew there was no way he was going to beat that Golden Retriever," she said, munching her sandwich and trying to ignore Sid, who was doing his best impression of a prizewinning dog who had never, ever been fed. "That was the soppiest dog I've ever seen."

"Even more lovey-dovey than Sid when he wants sandwiches," Dad agreed. "No, Sid. Not even for a champion red-rosette winner." He chuckled to himself. "I still can't believe you kept all of his tricks a secret, Bella. It was amazing."

Mum nodded. "I was so proud of you. Oh, it's nearly time for the 'Waggiest Tail' class."

Bella hauled Sarah up off the picnic
blanket, and Mum passed them Sid's
lead.

Bella looked thoughtfully at Sarah
as they walked across to the ring. Her
friend kept looking longingly at all
the dogs they went past. Bella hadn't
realized until now how much Sarah
must be missing her grandad's dog.
"Do you want to take Sid into this
class?" she asked suddenly. "I know

it's not the same as having Alfie, but I think you should. You worked on training him, too. And it was you who suggested we should look for a show with fun classes!"

"Can I really?" Sarah asked, her eyes shining excitedly.

Bella nodded. "Definitely. Sid loves you, so it won't bother him. Look, it's that same nice lady calling out the names. I'll explain to her – I'm sure she won't mind."

Bella pushed the lead into Sarah's hand and hurried over to the lady sitting in the corner of the ring to explain. She could see Sarah crouching next to Sid and stroking him lovingly, so she was sure she'd done the right thing.

Bella dashed back. "She says it's fine," she told Sarah. "The class is about to start — come on. Over here." Bella pushed Sarah into the right place in the line of dogs, and watched proudly as they all walked into the ring.

"Where's Sid?" Tom asked, looking

round worriedly as he and Mum and Dad came over.

"I let Sarah take him," Bella said. "You don't mind, do you? You did say you didn't want to be in the show."

Tom shuddered. "I definitely don't mind. Sid looks like he loves all the attention, but I'd hate it."

When it was Sarah and Sid's turn Sarah rubbed the perfect spot on Sid's spine, and he wagged his tail so hard he nearly fell over.

"And we have a clear winner there," called the announcer. "Yes, the judges are going for Sid! Handled by one of his best friends – Sarah! Well done, Sid and Sarah!"

Chapter Eight

Bella jumped up and down, clapping, and Sarah hurried back to her with scarlet cheeks, clutching another red rosette. "You won!" Bella hugged her. "You see, I knew I was right to get you to go in. Sid's a champion. Two firsts!"

"What's the next class, Bella?" Tom asked. "Whatever it is, I think your friend Megan's in it." He pointed across the ring to where Megan was lining up with Coco. "Oh, 'Cutest Puppy Under Nine Months'. Well, she is cute. She doesn't look very happy about it, though."

Coco was pulling, and pawing at her lead, as though she wanted to get away. Megan was trying to calm her down, but she looked worried, too, and Coco was whimpering.

"Poor thing, I don't think she likes how noisy it is," Bella said anxiously. "Oh no!"

Coco had been pulling and scrabbling at her collar so much, and now she slipped right out of it. She stood there for a second, looking bewildered by her sudden freedom and the noise. Megan tried to grab her, but a little boy screamed because he'd dropped his ice cream, and Coco shot away with a squeak. She bolted along the side of the ring towards Bella and Sarah, and then darted out through a forest of feet and off into the rest of the field.

"Coco!" Megan wailed, dashing after her, but she was blocked by all the other handlers and dogs going into the ring.

"We have to help catch her!" Bella gasped. "Look after Sid, Sarah." She pushed and squeezed her way through the crowd of people and looked around anxiously for Coco.

The little spaniel was cowering by the side of an ice-cream van, obviously terrified. Bella walked over to her, trying to be slow and gentle – she really wanted to grab Coco before she ran off again, but if she moved too fast, she'd just frighten her away.

"Dog treats!" Bella gasped, realizing she still had half the pack in her pocket. "Hey, Coco… Look what I've got." She held out a few, rattling them gently and murmuring some soothing words to the nervous little spaniel. "Pretty girl, yes, look. Yummy treats. Pretty Coco, come on then…"

Coco eyed her worriedly, but she could smell the treats, and the girl's voice was gentle, not cross. She wanted

Megan, but she was frightened of all the noise, and she didn't dare go back and find her. She crept slowly forward and sniffed at Bella's hand, and then she started to nibble at the crunchy biscuits.

Bella ran a gentle hand over Coco's head, still murmuring soothing words, and then as the puppy munched the last of the treats, Bella picked her up.

Coco wriggled a little, but Bella was holding her carefully, tight enough that she couldn't squirm away.

"We need to find Megan, and your collar," she whispered. "Hey, look, Coco, there she is!"

Megan was racing towards them, with tears running down her cheeks. As soon as Coco saw her, she wriggled eagerly, stretching out of Bella's arms to reach her. Megan hugged her, and Coco licked her chin, and nuzzled at her neck. Bella laughed – Coco might not like the dog show, but it was obvious she adored Megan.

"I thought I'd never find her!" Megan said gratefully, looking at Bella. "You must have run after her really fast. I was worried she might get into the car park." She shuddered, and Bella put an arm round her shoulders.

"It's OK, we got her back. Here, let's put her collar on again." Bella helped Megan to fasten it, and Bella put Coco down gently. Then she glanced back up at Megan.

"I'm really sorry I agreed with Lara about Sid," Megan said. "I was so horrible. And to Sarah, too. It's just, I never thought we wouldn't be friends, and then suddenly you were with *her* all the time…"

"She's nice. A lot nicer than Lara and Chloe," Bella said. "I still like you, but I don't want to hang around with them any more."

Megan looked at her feet. "I know. I don't like them much either. But if you aren't friends with Lara, she says bad things about you…"

Bella shrugged. "I don't care." And she didn't, she realized. She probably would, when Lara started up again, but she would tell herself that it didn't really matter. "We can just walk away," she pointed out to Megan.

"I suppose so. I'll say sorry to Sarah." Megan looked at her hopefully. "Do you think we can go back to being friends?"

Bella smiled. "We could try…"

"How did you get Sid to do that amazing walking on his hind paws?" Megan asked, as they wandered along the path through the park.

It was Sunday afternoon, and Bella had arranged for her and Megan and Sarah and their mums to meet up. She was a bit worried about Megan and Sarah not getting on, so she wanted them to try and get to know each other, before they all had to go back to school on Monday.

"You saw that?" Bella asked, feeling pleased. "It's all about dog treats. Sid's really greedy. He'd do anything for them."

"I wonder if Coco could." Megan sighed. "She's lovely, but I'm not very good at getting her to do what she's told."

"She is only little," Sarah pointed out. "She'll probably get more sensible as she gets older."

"Maybe… But I wish she'd hurry up," Megan sighed. "She keeps eating things. One of my mum's shoes yesterday."

"Why don't you bring her to the dog-training classes at the church hall?" Bella suggested. "We're starting to go next week."

Megan looked hopeful. "That's a good idea. Is the class OK for beginners, too? I mean, Sid's already so good."

Bella glowed. He *was* good. He was fabulous, actually. "I'm sure it's all right," she agreed proudly, watching Sid and Coco walking sweetly next to each other.

"They look like friends already,"

Sarah said, laughing at them. "Look, they're chatting."

Bella looked over. It was true. Sid and Coco were standing with their heads together, watching a jogger speeding down the path towards them. They looked so cute beside each other.

"I don't think they like his orange trainers," Megan whispered, and Bella tried not to laugh. It felt good, being with Megan and Sarah. And Coco and Sid obviously loved walking together, as well.

"They're definitely friends," Bella said, smiling at Megan. She didn't need to say it, but what she really meant was, *We all are...*

HOLLY WEBB

Holly Webb started out as a children's book editor and wrote her first series for the publisher she worked for. She has been writing ever since, with over one hundred books to her name. Holly lives in Berkshire, with her husband and three children. Holly's pet cats are always nosying around when she is trying to type on her laptop.

For more informatio
about Holly Webb

www.holly-v